SEE A PENNY

Tessa and Matthew have shared a close bond since childhood. When he asks her to marry him to keep her safe while he is away in the RAF she knows it is nothing more than friendship. But when Matthew's air-base is bombed Tessa realises how much she loves him. Her letters to him go unanswered as she is caught up in the death and destruction of the Blitz. Will Tessa and Matthew find their way back to each other?

SALLY HAWKER

◆

SEE A PENNY

Complete and Unabridged

LINFORD
Leicester

First published in Great Britain in 2011

First Linford Edition
published 2021

A catalogue record for this book is available
from the British Library.

ISBN 978–1–4448–4720–8

Published by
Ulverscroft Limited
Anstey, Leicestershire

Printed and bound in Great Britain by
TJ Books Ltd., Padstow, Cornwall

This book is printed on acid-free paper

Just Another War Bride

August 1939

Twisting first to one side and then the other, Tessa Thorne surveyed her reflection in the gilt-edged mirror that hung above Bea's dressing table.

With a critical eye, she peered at the delicate cream lace stitched so intricately around the neckline of the dress she wore as to suggest it had always been there, the pretty lace that had transformed a simple white cotton frock into a gown fit for a bride.

'You look smashing, Tess.' Beatrice Cooper, with whom she'd been friends since childhood, smiled a watery smile, her eyes brimming with unshed tears.

'Oh, Bea, don't start blubbing,' Tessa chided. 'Not quite love's young dream, is it? All this palaver just so Matthew can keep me here and tied to his ma's apron strings ...'

1

'So he can keep you safe, more like,' Bea cut in. 'Word on our base is that they'll start calling up women soon, and them without a ring on their finger and no ties to speak of will be the first to go.'

Tessa turned from the mirror, her expression wistful as she perched for a minute on the edge of Bea's bed.

'I'm no coward, Bea. I never said I wouldn't do my bit. Half of me thinks I should have enrolled with you and be down in Norfolk learning to man barrage balloons.'

For a minute Bea returned the same wistful smile, both of them thinking of how, after the trouble in Munich the year before, since it had become increasingly clear that the country was headed into war, they'd talked of joining the Women's Auxiliary Air Force, and how they'd planned to join up together.

But although Bea was stationed at Coltishall air base, receiving her training, Tessa was still here, in Birmingham.

She was doing her bit for the War effort, admittedly, since the clothing factory at which she and Bea had worked since leaving school had been turned over to the production of military uniforms, but there was seldom a day went past when Tessa didn't feel a pang of remorse that her dear friend had bravely volunteered for the front line while she was in the relatively safe surroundings of the city that was the only home she'd ever known.

'Don't be daft.' Bea reached for Tessa's hand and squeezed it gently.

'Not exactly a holiday camp in that there factory, is it? Still, labour of love for some of us, I reckon.' There was a twinkle in her eye as she continued. 'All this palaver indeed. And you frowning over that lace as if you didn't stitch every inch yourself. You know it looks exquisite.'

Tessa allowed herself one more admiring glance in the mirror before she took the small posy of chrysanthemums Bea held out to her.

'Scrubs up all right, I suppose.'

'You look smashing,' Bea repeated solemnly, herding her friend towards the door. 'Come on, we'll be late and Esme will be in even more of a lather.'

'She'll be in a lather anyway.' Tessa grimaced at the thought of the opposition Esme Lane felt towards her son's choice of bride, feelings she never made any attempt to conceal.

'You don't need her approval,' Bea reasoned. 'If you ask me, that's half what's up with her. You and Matthew all grown up and out from under her eagle eye. She's no control any more and she knows it.'

'Not over us, in any case,' Tessa pondered, as Bea gave her a little push towards the stairs.

'Come on, girl. Some of us are wanted back at barracks by tonight. Let's get you married while I'm still here to see it.'

From the cramped lodgings above the pawnbroker's that Bea shared with her ma, Dorrie, and Bertie, her twin brother, the walk to the register office took only a matter of minutes.

Bea suggested taking a more circuitous route to allow for the traditional lateness that was a bride's prerogative and Esme could like it or lump it, but for Tessa, pandering to such romantic nonsense was pointless under the circumstances.

Due back at the factory this afternoon, she had no time to dally. Dorrie Cooper was the gaffer in charge of her line and had offered to swing it so she could take the whole day; after all, it was her wedding day and just the morning off hardly seemed fair; but Tessa had assured her that it was all she needed.

On Dorrie's face she'd read a fleeting pity that what should be the most important day in a girl's life Tessa was discarding so matter-of-factly. She knew, as they all did, the reason Matthew Lane had for making Tessa his wife, but like her daughter, Bea, Dorrie seemed at a loss to understand that there could be nothing more to it.

Tessa knew they felt sad for her that her wedding day should be viewed so mechanically, so coldly, that she should stand before the registrar with a man she didn't love, at least in that way, but to her, and to Matthew, they had the best reason in the world to do it.

He'd been her best friend for as long she could remember. When Tessa's pa had returned from the Great War with injuries so grave he'd been admitted to the infirmary on several occasions, he'd lived long enough to see his daughter born, after which his wife had managed the first few months of Tessa's life before she'd followed him into the ground, leaving her daughter to the mercy of Esme Lane, who lived next door.

But it was Hilary, Matthew's elder sister, who had, for the most part, raised Tessa, and Matthew too, when Esme had responded to her own husband's death not much above a year later by taking root in his armchair, leaving the running of the house to her quietly spoken, but very efficient daughter.

Hillie had been the closest thing to a mother Tessa had known, despite there being only eight years between them. But she'd had her cantankerous ma to run around after as well, and Tessa and

Matthew had quickly grown accustomed to looking after each other.

Just as they were doing now, Tessa thought, as she and Bea approached the cold, stone steps of the register office.

They'd taken a tram out to the Lickeys, the day he asked her to marry him.

With Tessa working her fingers to the bone at the factory and Matthew doing overtime on the buses, it was rare that they had an afternoon off together but when they did, they often headed out to the hills on the edge of the city.

Matthew had stretched out on the grass, his jacket folded into a cushion behind his head as he dozed in the sunshine, sitting beside him and embroidering a pattern of forget-me-not flowers into the handkerchief she'd sewn for Bea, Tessa had felt as contented as she'd believed it was possible to feel.

She'd known then that Matthew planned to sign up for the Royal Air Force of his own accord and she was frightened for him, but at that moment he was asleep beside her and she could see he was safe. For the time being she'd felt perfectly at ease.

But Matthew hadn't been asleep. He'd been thinking, and moments later he'd opened his eyes, sat up, and took her hand in his.

At first she'd told him not to be daft. He was her best friend, yes, and the most important person in her life, as she was to him, but they didn't love each other, not in the way they should if they were headed for the altar.

Matthew had been undeterred in the usual quiet manner that was like his sister, but with steely resolve that shone in his eyes he'd laid before Tessa the reasoning he'd been carefully thinking through for days.

Like Bea, Matthew had heard of the likely conscription of women into the forces, the general consensus being that those who were single and free of responsibilities would likely be called up first.

Officially an orphan, regardless of how inherent a part of the Lane family Tessa had grown to be, and with her willingness to join the W.A.A.F., chances are she'd be amongst the first wave to go.

Matthew was adamant that she should stay here, safe, at least for now, in the home she knew, and making her his wife, and an official Lane, was the most fail-safe way he could think of to do this.

'Our Hillie will be up and off any day now,' he'd reasoned, though they both knew that the chances of Hilary walking out on her mother were slim, no matter how keen Leo, her husband, was to find a house for them both and their daughter, Victoria. 'With Ma's chest as weak as it is, she'll need looking after.'

Tessa had smiled wryly at the thought. 'We'll be hard pushed to find a willing volunteer for that job, even if we scour the whole of Brum.'

He'd caught her eye and they'd shared a despairing look at how much more impossible Esme grew with every day she spent barking orders from the depths of her Arthur's armchair.

Tessa knew Matthew would never expect her to look after his ma single-handedly; nor did she for one minute take offence at how blithely he appeared to disregard her plans to enrol with the Women's Air Force; because she knew that his proposal, as sudden and unexpected as it was, came from the same place as everything else Matthew Lane said or did.

Since they'd been old enough to hold hands and scramble over the doorstep into the enticing freedom of Esme's back garden and the world beyond, they'd looked after each other, Matthew squaring up to anyone or anything he thought might threaten his Tessa.

Now they'd reached twenty-one, childhood scuffles in the street had been replaced by the war that everyone said was on its way, and Matthew was even more determined to protect her.

She could see how important it was to him, which in turn made it equally important to her. Matthew would be off soon to fight for his country. She couldn't keep him safe in the same way, but if she married him first, he'd belong to her, officially, as no-one else did.

She'd lost her ma when she was just a babby — surely after that she was owed the return of Matthew safe and in one piece.

Within minutes of ascending the steps into the cold, grey building that housed the register office, Tessa was standing beside Matthew, the monotonous tones of the registrar seeming to float somewhere above her. He seemed bored, she noticed, and perhaps he was, with the sudden rush of couples eager to introduce a bit of stability to their lives before the onset of war put miles and possibly even oceans between them.

'Easy as popping to the shop for a pint o' milk,' Esme muttered as Matthew solemnly slid a simple gold band on to Tessa's finger. 'Not even in a proper church, neither ...'

Tessa had no need to glance back over her shoulder to know that Hilary would be clutching her ma's arm and attempting to quieten her with the infinite patience that never seemed to deplete no matter how awkwardly Esme behaved. She knew, too, that the old lady would shake off her daughter's ministrations as irritably as she might shake off a persistent fly. Esme relied wholeheartedly on Hilary, but she'd go to her grave having never admitted it!

It was Bertie Cooper, Bea's brother and Matthew's best man, who turned briefly to the woman he treated with an easy familiarity after the years he'd spent as a child, along with Bea, playing in the Lane's garden or in the street outside while Dorrie had been working long shifts at the factory.

Those who lived with Esme had learned to watch what they said in her hearing, if for no other reason than a quiet life for all concerned, but Bertie Cooper was a straight-forward chap, always ready with a smile as he strolled through life with a natural exuberance he extended to all, including Esme Lane, who Tessa suspected rather enjoyed the chance to spar with someone not so readily quashed by her acid tongue.

'Give over, our Esme.' Bertie flashed her the cheeky grin that was his trademark. 'You and me's only here for the free cake, remember?'

'Free to you, it might be, my lad,' Esme retorted. 'Wasn't paid for out o' your pocket, was it?'

'Nor out o' yours,' Bertie quipped, as the registrar closed his book with a dull thud, the tedious monotony of a steady stream of rushed unions giving way to a mild irritation that such an occasion should be marred by the best man bickering with the groom's mother! At once he began to not so furtively glance at his watch, but such pointed behaviour was unnecessary as none of them wished, or had time, to linger.

Turning to smile at Tessa, Matthew tucked her hand under his arm and the two of them led the way outside into the mid-morning sunshine. In an hour or two Tessa was due back at her sewing machine, Matthew had an afternoon shift driving the Selly Oak bus route, Bea

13

had to catch a train back down to Nor-folk, Bertie was expected out on a job with the Gas Board and Leo, Hilary's husband, though he had a little more time at his disposal, was scheduled to work a late shift in the North signal box at New Street station; but first they were walking back to Esme's house where the wedding breakfast Hilary had prepared was waiting for them.

They made for a funny little group, Tessa mused, as they strolled along the pavement. She and Matthew walked a little way apart from the rest, as they'd been prone to do since childhood, with Bea closing the gap as she was persuaded to break into a skip by Victoria, who had her hand firmly clasped in Aunty Bea's.

Behind them Leo and Bertie walked at a more sedate pace, talking and nod-ding together over something, and bringing up the rear with the slow and stiff movements her nearest and dearest knew to be at least a little exaggerated, was Esme, the grand matriarch of her extended family unit, leaning heavily on her Hillie's arm.

'We've gone and done it now, then,' Matthew said quietly. 'Any regrets, Tess?'

'Only one.' She turned to smile at him, dispelling the brief flutter of anxiety in his eyes. 'I'm Mrs Lane now, same as your ma.'

Matthew's eyes sparkled as he reflected her smile. 'So long as I don't come home to find you've taken root in that old armchair.'

'So long as you come home,' she repeated softly, the familiar dark fear beginning to twist her stomach, and he placed his hand, briefly over hers, both of them relieved to have something else to divert their thoughts when Victoria broke free of Bea's hand and dived to the pavement where she scooped up something into her hand with a squeal of triumph.

'See a penny, pick it up; all day long you'll have good luck!'

She bounded up to Tessa and Matthew, her little face shining.

'Give me your hand, Tess.'

Obediently, Tessa held out her palm, into which Victoria carefully placed the penny on which she'd pounced.

'Better than treasure, that is,' she declared, with the insight of a child far beyond her eight years. 'It's a lucky penny, see? For you and Uncle Matthew, to keep you safe for ever.'

Tessa closed her fingers over the precious penny. 'Thank you,' she said softly, and Victoria beamed with pride that was only slightly dimmed when Grandma Esme's acerbic tones drifted across the distance between them.

'Scavenging in the gutter for coppers now, is she? Our Vic's taking after the wrong one, Hillie. You can dress her up in that fancy frock, but it don't make no difference. Taking after Tessa, she is. Sharp as sixpence and a right little tomboy.

'As for Madam, she's lucky our Mattie's put that ring on her finger. Not many lads hereabouts will be wanting to wed a lass who's spent more time up to her ears in muck than they have ... '

Rolling her eyes at Tessa, Bea reclaimed Victoria's hand, the pair of them skipping on ahead.

Tessa tightened her fingers around the penny until the cold hardness of it dug painfully into her skin. She didn't tend to hold much with what she saw as superstitious nonsense, though of course she'd cut out her own tongue before she uttered one word to hurt Victoria's feelings, but she found now that she wanted desperately to believe that all it would take to bring Matthew safely home was one little lucky penny.

'You'd best keep hold of that then,' Matthew murmured, for a brief second the fear Tessa felt mirrored in his hazel eyes.

★   ★   ★

Marrying her best friend had been just another day, much like all the others once she'd changed out of her posh frock and swept her long, glossy auburn hair back under the floral scarf she wore to protect it from getting caught up in the sewing machine.

With the pace at which Dorrie Cooper worked her girls, as used to it as Tessa was, half a day had tired her almost as much as the normal ten hour shift, so that by the time she returned home, she was too weary to care about anything besides a cup of tea and her bed.

In the dim light given off by the one gas lamp in the back room that, along with a poky little kitchen, comprised their living space, Tessa sat and drank tea with Hilary, who was waiting up for Leo to return from his shift, as she always did, even when he wasn't expected back through the door until the small hours.

They kept their conversation to a murmur, having no wish to wake Esme; who was dozing in her chair. A martyr to the numerous aches and pains she claimed were ailing her more fiercely with every day that passed, Esme might have been wise to retire to the front room, her parlour as she grandly referred to it, in which she slept so as to free up the three bedrooms upstairs for her family, but she insisted on remaining in her chair by the fire for as long as it took for the last inhabitant of her cramped little terraced house to walk back through the door.

'Terrified o' missing summat, she is,' Leo had been heard to mutter on more than one occasion, and Tessa and Matthew knew, if Hilary didn't, or as was more likely, pretended she didn't, that Leo Rawlins was growing increasingly jaded at the omnipresence of his mother-in-law.

It wasn't unreasonable to expect that he and Hilary and Victoria should be thinking about moving out into their own house; indeed the Corporation kept a list of young families in just such a situation, who were waiting for a property to rent.

Leo had tentatively broached the subject with Hilary, suggesting that they at least put their names down; after all, vacant properties in their area — for he knew better than to ask his Hillie to put too much space between herself and her mother — were so few and far between that there were some families who had been kept waiting for months and still were; but Hilary had refused to so much as contemplate the idea and Leo, who loved his wife so much he backed down instantly rather than cause her further distress, was stuck under the same roof as his cantankerous mother-in-law for the foreseeable future.

'Victoria was ever so pleased she found that penny for you, Tess,' Hilary said, her voice barely above a whisper as she smiled fondly. 'You know she believes in that silly old rhyme?'

'If it keeps Matthew safe, then so do I,' Tessa replied simply, and Hilary reached across the table to pat her hand.

'Where's he got to, anyway? Shift finished by now, hasn't it? Or has he got a bit of overtime?'

Tessa shook her head. 'He's at the Black Horse. Bertie's playing there tonight. Matthew said he'd stop by for a drink after work.'

'Did he now?' Hilary tutted quietly.

'Fine way to see out his wedding day, that is.'

'You know how it is, Hillie,' Tessa reminded her. 'We're wed in name only. He's no need to be at my side constantly.'

'Ring on your finger changed the habit of a lifetime, then, has it?' Hilary looked at her new sister-in-law, her expression grave in the flickering light the gas lamp threw across them. 'If nothing else you pair were always thick as thieves and not an inch of daylight between you. Madly in love you may not be but I know you love him as your closest ally, Tess, as he does you. When's he off?'

'Monday week.' Tessa squeezed her eyes shut briefly, fighting against the dark terror that threatened to overwhelm her when she thought of Matthew going off to train with the Royal Air Force.

'A matter of days, then.' Hilary's own voice trembled and she took a mouthful of tea in an attempt to compose herself. 'If for no other reason he should be here with those he loves best. Goodness knows, that Bertie one manages to drum up enough of a devoted audience hanging off his every note without Matthew needing to lead the applause.'

'He plays that piano like a pro,' Tessa said, pleased to have lighter thoughts on which to dwell, but Hilary was not so easily diverted, her own fear suddenly visible in her expressive hazel eyes, and Tessa knew she was thinking not so much of Matthew's fate but of Leo's.

As determined as Matthew was to do his bit, Leo had enrolled with the Territorial Army some months previously, a commitment which took up one evening a week and every other weekend, fitting around his job on the railway and providing a little more respite from his mother-in-law, though he'd never say as much to Hilary.

His training recently completed, Leo had emerged a fully fledged soldier, available to be despatched at a moment's notice should the order come. Tessa knew Hilary, if not Leo himself, was living in fear of what seemed to be the inevitable eventual summons.

'He's not been called up yet,' she reasoned softly. 'He'll come home tonight, Hillie.'

Hilary managed to smile bravely, getting to her feet and absorbing herself in the task of putting the pot back on to boil as they heard the familiar sound of Matthew's footsteps down the side alley that led into the garden and the back door.

Knowing his ma would be dozing in her chair, as her failing health caused her to do most evenings now, Matthew took care to let himself in as quietly as he could, having no more wish than the girls to wake Esme, but the old lady's hearing was one faculty that was still as sharp as it had been when she was a lass, and she was sitting up and muttering to Hilary to hurry up with that there tea before Matthew had so much as taken his boots off.

'Where'd you get to then, my lad?' Esme demanded, as if Matthew was still a small boy needing to be scolded for playing out late rather than the twenty-one year old man who raised an eyebrow at her as he sank down into a chair.

'Been running amok through the streets of Brum with a bucket of paint and a brush but never fear, Ma, the law won't come knocking. I've dumped it all in the cut, done away with the evidence, see.'

'Laughing on t'other side of your face, you'd be, if someone had done that and the constable happened to pass and hear you boasting of it,' Esme stated imperiously, turning her scathing glare on to Tessa, who'd failed to hide the smile behind her cup. 'As for you, Madam, feeling pleased with yourself, are you? Getting my lad to put a ring on your finger when there's all manner o' pretty girls hereabouts — he could have had his pick!'

'I didn't get him to do anything,' Tessa returned stiffly, but the words were barely out of her mouth before Matthew startled them all by banging his fist down on to the table.

'Leave her alone, Ma. Tessa and I are

wed. If you don't like it, you'll have to lump it.'

'Matthew!' Hilary pleaded softly, her expressive hazel eyes pools of apprehension at the thought that there might be upset. 'You'll wake Victoria if you carry on like that.'

'Sorry, Hillie.' Matthew took the cup she passed to him, making an obvious effort to swallow back any further words he might have aimed at his ma, but she was not so prepared to draw a line under it.

'Not a proper marriage anyway,' she muttered. 'Moment of foolishness, brought on by this war folk say is round the comer, and you flitting off to play at being a pilot. Followed your pa on to the buses and now your set on following him into an early grave ...'

'Esme! Please!' This time it was Tessa who snapped, a little of her tea spilling over into the saucer as she slammed it down and faced her mother-inlaw. 'How can you even think such a thing, let alone speak the words?'

'Tess, it's all right.' Matthew placed a hand comfortingly on her arm, and suddenly conscious of Hilacy's stricken face not to mention the fact that Victoria was asleep upstairs, Tessa turned away from Esme, struggling to regain her composure for she was shaking with anger.

'Bertie raised a crowd and a half tonight,' Matthew said, to no-one in particular. 'Had a whip round, they did, too. Made a packet at last count.'

Quick to follow his lead and establish a bit of calm, Hilary spoke with a brightness Tessa knew was at least partly forced.

'What's that towards, then?'

But here Matthew hesitated, giving Esme time to put in her two-penceworth.

'Lining his pockets, I shouldn't wonder. As if folk ain't got better to spend their money on in this day and age.'

'It's for the children, actually, Ma,' Matthew corrected her, and as he continued to explain which children and why. Tessa knew the cause of his earlier hesitation in revealing to Hilary the details of what he'd initially leapt upon as a convenient change of subject without thinking through the consequences.

With the whole of Brum buzzing with whispered fears of enemy landings, of bombs and the dreaded gas attacks, for some time now, folk were aware too of the proposed plans to evacuate as many children as possible to the safety of the countryside.

It seemed Bertie and his pals had hit upon the idea of raising a bit of money that could be used to purchase in bulk little treats that might make such a harrowing experience a touch more bearable; an assortment of toys, perhaps, or a tray of cakes from the bakery, iced specially.

'Anyone would think it were a day out to the fair,' Esme muttered. 'Carted off to the countryside, they ain't about to give two figs for a fairy cake, even if it's iced so thick it rots every tooth!'

'Poor little mites,' Hilary put in softly, and it was clear from those three little words that her mind instinctively balked at placing Victoria amongst them.

'You'd be wise to send our Vic along with them,' Esme told her bluntly.

'Unless you want her here at the mercy o' them bombs and the like.'

Hilary shook her head, for a moment unable to speak, and Matthew, seeing how his sister struggled to order her thoughts, diverted the wrath of Esme back onto his own shoulders.

'You just want our Hillie at your beck and call, isn't that the way of it, Ma? You ship Victoria off to the country and with Leo likely to be called up, you get the good of Hillie's undivided attention ...'

Incredibly tired suddenly and unable for one moment longer to bear such a conversation which in her mind was inextricably linked with Matthew's imminent departure, Tessa mumbled her goodnights and trudged wearily up the stairs to the small room she shared with Victoria.

Despite the raised tempers downstairs, the child was sleeping soundly, but with

28

an instinctive silence borne of years of practice, Tessa undressed and climbed into bed without making a sound.

She was so weary her mind screamed to slip into blissful oblivion but, almost as if she could hear the dull tick of the minutes passing and bringing closer the moment she'd have to watch Matthew get onto a train, she lay awake in the darkness, nervously twisting the ring on her finger, for some hours before sleep finally claimed her.

* * *

She'd been a married woman only a little above a week when she stood on a platform at New Street station, clutching Matthew's sleeve, partly to keep him by her side for as log as possible and partly to hold on to him amongst the jostling throng of folk who filled the platform to bursting, all it seemed, facing similarly painful goodbyes.

'Least you'll get your marriage allowance from the services now,' Matthew said with a brightness Tessa knew was forced. 'King's ransom of a pound a week, you'll be set up for life.'

She shook her head numbly. She was determined she wouldn't cry and make this any harder for them.

'It'll be all right, Tess.' Matthew's tone was softer as he looked at her. 'You know I'll be back. Like the proverbial bad penny.' He managed a thin smile. 'Keep it safe and I will too. Wise head on her shoulders, that Victoria's got.'

Tessa forced herself to smile too, but it was so incredibly hard. 'You're my best friend in the world,' she told him, unable now to stop her voice trembling. 'I can't imagine life without you.'

'Then don't,' he muttered fiercely. 'You've no need to.'

As the guard started waving people onto the train, Matthew pulled Tessa close to him, holding her tightly for a brief moment before he loosened his grip and, as if he could bear it no longer, planted a quick kiss on the top of her head and then shouldered his kitbag.

In seconds he was gone, swallowed up by the crowd.

By candlelight Tessa worked into the small hours that night. Long after Hilary and everyone else had retired to bed, she sat at the table, poring over every little stitch until finally it was finished. Blowing out the candle, she went silently up the stairs to her bedroom, where in the darkness she felt around in the drawer until her fingers closed around the lucky penny. She placed it carefully into the tiny muslin pouch, pulling the ribbon tight to secure it before stowing it away safely at the back of her drawer.

Comings and Goings

One of the first out the factory gates
come clocking off time, Tessa was hurry-
ing along the street before she'd finished
buckling the belt of her light gabardine
coat.

Lately she'd taken to allowing herself
a more circular route home, one which
took her through the park and even at
the briskest pace added a good ten minutes to her journey, delaying her return
to the house that didn't feel as it once
had, not without Matthew there, but
this evening her conscience forbade her
to dally.

Tomorrow morning she was to take
Victoria to New Street station, where
she'd be joining the hundreds of other
children bound for the promised safety
of living amongst strangers in the country.

It would mean taking an hour off work,
of course, and Dorrie Cooper, though

she'd never think of refusing given the circumstances, had been confused as to why Victoria's mother was not escorting the child herself, especially as she'd no work commitments as such.

Loyalty to Hilary had deterred Tessa from venting the frustration she felt herself on this point, and so she'd merely offered the rather flimsy explanation that her sister-in-law found the thought of waving Victoria off at the station far too painful, and with Leo due on a shift in the signal box, it had fallen to Tessa to step in and do the honours.

Hilary would find it incredibly painful, of course, as would the hundreds of other mothers in the same position, a fair few of whom Tessa thought wryly would nonetheless grip small hands in theirs until they had no choice but to let go. Not for one moment did she believe that Hilary loved Victoria any less than this, but with Esme clamouring for *her Hillie* to be at her beck and call every hour of the day, there was only so much of herself Hilary could give.

In her sister-in-law's eyes that couldn't quite meet hers, Tessa had glimpsed an overwhelming guilt, put there by the old woman dozing in the corner and for what wasn't the first time, nor would it be the last, she'd felt so sorry for Hillie, for whom marriage to Leo and even the birth of their child had failed to bring independence from her ma.

It was Esme who'd talked her into sending Victoria off with the rest. When they'd heard for definite that a first wave of children were to be evacuated from Birmingham on the first day of September, Hilary and Leo had been united in their decision that Victoria should stay with them; after all, who better to protect her from harm than her own parents?

But then Esme had set to work, bit by bit dropping pointed comments and more often than not direct arguments, until she had Hilary convinced of the sense in sending Victoria off to live with strangers, and Leo, despite his anger, was less inclined than ever to argue with his wife, given that he'd likely be called up sooner rather than later. If they were down to what could feasibly be their last days together, he'd no thought to spending them in conflict.

Nevertheless, the atmosphere in that little back room would be fraught at the very least this evening, Tessa thought grimly as she hurried along the side passage and round to the back door.

For the sake of Hilary, who'd be emotional but struggling to conceal it, and Victoria, who'd been incredibly brave thus far but who would surely falter a little given the immineilce of her departure, Tessa was determined to be the best support she could.

'Letter for you on the side, Tess.' Hilary glanced up from the stove, where she was stirring a pan of potatoes, and smiled distractedly. 'Definitely my brother's illegible scrawl.'

Everything else forgotten for a minute, Tessa crossed to the mantel above the fire, retrieving the envelope addressed to her from where it had been placed behind the clock for safe keeping.

35

Matthew had been away for more than a week now, and this was the first she'd heard from him. He'd warned her it may take a while before he was at liberty to put pen to paper, or even until he was of a fixed abode that he could give her an address safe in the knowledge that, for the time being at least, he'd not be moved on to anywhere else, but her logical mind had failed to override the sick feeling of disappointment with each day she'd returned home from work to find that the post had still brought no news of Matthew.

Now, at last, she held his letter in her hand.

'Too much trouble to address it to all of us,' Esme muttered from her armchair. 'Making his own ma wait to hear what's become of him 'til Lady Muck herself waltzes in ...'

Tessa found it unusually easy to shut her mind to the old lady's ramblings as she sat stiffly in a chair and read Matthew's letter. Coming to the end of it, she looked up to see Hilary hovering by the table, concern in her eyes for her little brother. For Hilary's sake rather than Esme's, Tessa relayed the contents.

'He's all right, Hillie. He's stationed at an air base in Norfolk — West Raynham, it's called — he's being trained up for ground crew.'

Hilary smiled the relief that Tessa felt that, as yet, Matthew wouldn't be taking to the danger of the skies, but Esme's tone was scathing as she put in her twopence worth.

'What happened to being a pilot, then? Royal Ground Force, now, is it? Still, it's unnatural if you ask me, men messing about in planes and the like. Birds are meant to fly and them with two feet should be keeping 'em on the ground.'

'Then you've nothing to condemn him for, have you?' Tessa sighed, refolding the letter and slipping it carefully back into the envelope. She'd stow it away in her drawer, with the pouch containing their lucky penny.

Esme's steel-grey eyes glinted fury at the one 'daughter' who wasn't so quick to mind what she said.

'Norfolk, then,' she continued, her pointed tone making Tessa glance up at her sharply. 'Isn't that where Bea is?'

'They're stationed at different bases, Esme.'

'Handy, though, being so close, them being pals and all. They'll be going to dances and the like, I imagine. No stopping them, like.'

Knowing what she was implying, Tessa counted to ten in her head before she answered. Esme wanted a reaction, but she'd not give her the satisfaction.

'It's not a jolly holiday at the seaside, but yes, I suppose they might cross paths at some point, and if it lifts their spirits to see a friendly face then I hope they do.'

'Sanctity o' marriage,' Esme muttered, determined as she always was to steal the last word. 'Meaning of it's lost on you pair. Saying your vows when they mean nowt, and you turning a blind eye to our Mattie whirling Bea, and others, too, I shouldn't wonder, round that dance floor like he's clean forgot he put that ring on your finger.'

'There's no harm in him dancing,' Tessa began, but knowing she was being drawn into an argument, she clamped her mouth shut, instead rising to her feet to take Matthew's letter upstairs. For Hilary's sake, Victoria's, too, she'd keep quiet ... for now.

'In my day wedding vows meant something, and it weren't just a means o' getting a roof over your head ...'

Esme's scathing tone floated after Tessa as she trudged up the stairs to the room she shared with her niece.

Victoria was sitting cross-legged on her bed, with her battered little suitcase open in front of her. Inside her clothes had been neatly folded, with a space alongside left in which to squeeze Billy Bear, the threadbare teddy she'd had since she was a babby, but as yet he was lying in her lap, staring up at her out of expressionless button eyes as she carefully tied the blue ribbon around his neck into a perfect bow.

'Billy looks smart,' Tessa said, and Victoria smiled bravely.

'He's to look his best so we get picked to live with somebody nice.'

With Matthew's letter stowed safely away in her drawer, Tessa sat on the edge of her own bed; opposite Victoria, whose eyes shone not so much with the usual courage but with the tell-tale sign of recently shed tears.

'There'll be someone there whose job it is to see that you get put with someone nice,' Tessa told her gently. 'You've no need to fret that you won't get picked.'

Victoria looked up at her. 'I heard Granny say to Ma that she'd better mind I was in one of my nice frocks and make sure I knew I weren't to get it mucky, else no-one would want me going home and staying with them.'

Tessa swallowed the anger that rose in her throat. It would do Victoria no good were she to show it but then that child was so astute that glossing over it, or worse telling her a blatant lie, would be recognised as such.

'She wants the best for you, same as we all do,' she said 'She just has a way of putting it — sometimes the words don't come out right.'

'I'll say.' Victoria rolled her eyes, looking every inch a teenager twice her age. 'She don't even get my name right. 'Our Vic' she calls me. Makes me sound like a lad, Tess.'

Tessa smiled, throwing her a wink. 'Are you not a lad, then? Way you rattle around on that old go-cart of Matthew's, I was beginning to think you were!'

But Victoria refused to be placated. 'You don't like her calling Uncle Matthew 'Mattie',' she pointed out instead, and Tessa blinked at her in surprise. It was true, she didn't, but try as she might, she couldn't recall a time when she'd said as much to anyone.

'Do you and Uncle Matthew love each other now, then?' Victoria continued, her arms wrapped tightly around Billy Bear.

'We always have,' Tessa told her, though she knew that wasn't quite what Victoria meant, but it was no lie all the same. 'Since we were little and getting under your ma's feet every day.'

Sliding down from her own bed, Victoria climbed up on to Tessa's, in an uncharacteristic moment of vulnerability curling herself into her lap.

'Tell me about when you and Uncle Matthew steered the go-cart into the canal.'

Tessa wrapped one arm around her, the other hand stroking her soft curls as she retold the story Victoria already knew by heart.

'We took it down by the cut, even though your ma, and Granny, too, told us we'd to keep away from any water, but there's miles and miles of towpath and we couldn't resist it, so we went down there and we took it in turns pushing each other ...'

'Until the wheel fell off,' Victoria prompted.

'It was working itself loose anyway,' Tessa continued. 'We thought it would hold til we got home but it rolled over a big stone and it came off with such a big jolt that the go-cart flew straight into the cut, with me clinging to it for dear life!'

'And Uncle Matthew dived in after you ...'

'He did, yes, though he'd have been better off staying on dry land and hauling me out. Pair of us were in a right state, splashing around, trying to pull ourselves back up the bank. Weren't too deep at the edge, luckily, else we'd have been in a pickle. Anyway, we got out, and then we dragged the go-cart out too. Never did find that wheel, though. Still at the bottom of the cut it'll be, rotting away by now, I suppose.'

'Then you were scared of going home 'cause of what Granny would say.'

'We knew we'd be for it.' Tessa smiled fondly, in her mind's eye seeing herself and Matthew as dripping, bedraggled ten-year-olds, holding hands firmly in a gesture of unity as they dragged the sorry looking specimen that was their go-cart back to face the wrath of Esme.

'When you got back you copped it from Granny because you dripped puddles all over the kitchen floor,' Victoria concluded, and Tessa squeezed her tightly.

'You could tell this story better than me now.'

'Uncle Matthew married you to keep you safe, didn't he?' Victoria asked.

'So you could live here instead of having to go away like me. 'Cept this time he didn't have to jump in the cut to save you.'

She'd give anything for the extent of Matthew's duty by his king and country to comprise nothing more than a quick ducking in the canal, Tessa thought, squeezing her eyes tightly shut against the tears that threatened.

'You're a treasure, Victoria. Yes, Uncle Matthew married me to keep me safe. Just like your ma is sending you to the country because she wants to keep you safe and that's the best way she knows to do it.'

Victoria snuggled into Tessa's arms, like a babby, but when she spoke, her voice was steadier, the courage trickling back.

'I know, Tess.'

Hours later Tessa was once more standing forlornly on a platform at New Street, yet again one of many struggling to hold back the tears as the train moved out of the station, but just as she'd been when saying goodbye to Matthew, the uneasy feeling in the pit of her stomach compounded further by Victoria's departure had Tessa convinced there was no other soul in the whole of the crowd milling around her who could possibly understand how alone and desolate she felt. Only when the train had turned a corner did she begin the walk back to the factory, but her progress was halted almost immediately by a hand on her arm.

'Excuse me, I'm sorry to bother you, but you look a decent sort so I'm hoping you'll not take offence.'

Tessa turned to see a young woman, roughly the same age as herself she thought, but the disparity in their appearances was striking. Where Tessa was dressed for work, a cardigan she'd darned more times than she cared to remember thrown on over her beige overalls, and her hair swept up under a scarf, comparatively this woman was the picture of sophistication in a richly woven woollen coat, a silk scarf draped about her throat and a mohair beret perched rakishly on a head of glossy black hair that curled under at the ends in the sleek pageboy style favoured by some women.

All at once conscious of how shabby and poor she must look next to this glamorous individual, Tessa could only wonder at why she'd been singled out when, given the density of the crowd still filling the platform as the sheer number of them impeded a swift exit, surely there were folk around more of an equal social standing to the woman standing before her, waiting patiently for a response.

'Of course,' Tessa managed. 'How can I be of service?'

The young woman's face creased into a smile. 'By losing the airs and graces for a start. I'm no toff, much as I'm dressed like a dummy in a Parisian boutique.'

She held her hand out to shake Tessa's. 'Lillian Foster. Lil to those who don't run fast enough.'

'Tessa Lane,' Tessa replied. 'Tess.'

'Pleased to meet you, Tess.' Lillian Foster looked around her, a kind of excited wonder shining in her eyes, and Tessa was reminded of the way Victoria had gazed about her in awe the first time she'd been taken to a toy emporium.

'Are you needing to find a taxi?' Tessa prompted, as for the moment her new acquaintance seemed at a loss for words, and as the crowd arotind them began to thin out, she was very much aware that time was ticking by and Dorrie was expecting her back behind her sewing machine.

Lillian looked back at her, a little bewildered, as if she'd forgotten she was there. 'A taxi, yes. Grand idea, Tess. Can't say as I was relishing the prospect of carting this lot all the way there, though as yet I've no idea where 'there' might be, which, my dear Tess, is where you come in. She paused, stooping to pick up the suitcase at her feet. 'I'm hoping you might be able to direct me to a decent place I can stay. Nothing too fancy, a boarding house, perhaps.'

Tessa thought for a moment, her mind raking over possibilities. Despite Lillian's protestations to the contrary, the elegant way she was dressed must surely mean she was used to a certain standard, not quite reached by the many cheap and cheerful establishments that dotted the city.

'First place you can think of,' Lillian declared. 'So long as there's hot water and a friendly face it'll do for me.'

'There's a boarding house on Hockley Street,' Tessa ventured cautiously. 'Run by a Mrs Cirelli. Nice woman by all accounts, and she keeps a clean home.'

'Good enough for me,' Lillian beamed. 'Mrs Cirelli's on Hockley Street it is. Where you off to? Shall we share a taxi?'

Tessa shook her head quickly. 'Thank you, but I've not got far to walk.'

In truth she'd cross Hockley Street before she reached the factory but all the same it wasn't too far a walk, if she kept up a fair pace she'd be there in twenty minutes. It certainly wasn't worth shelling out hard earned pence on half of a taxi fare, even with how much later she'd be now after this further and unexpected delay.

She accompanied Lillian outside the station where she hailed her a taxi. As the driver hoisted her luggage into his car, Lillian clasped Tessa's hand once more before she permitted her to leave.

'Many thanks, Tessa Lane. Perhaps we'll cross paths again and you'll allow me to repay your kindness.'

It was on the tip of Tessa's tongue to protest that such gratitude wasn't necessary; all she'd done was give her the name of a reputable boarding house, any one of the folk milling around could have done the same; but then she caught a glimpse of something in Lillian's face that, for the second time since they'd met, reminded her of Victoria, a child destined to travel to a strange place where she knew no-one, as fleeting in Lillian's case as it was given the second it took her to paint on a confident smile once more, but Tessa had seen it nonetheless, and so she smiled and shook her hand.

'Black Horse Inn on Gerard Street. Saturday afternoons a friend of mine plays piano. I usually drop by on my way into town. If you're at a loose end you're welcome to join me.'

For the briefest of moments Lillian Foster was once more the lost child smiling with relief at having found a trustworthy hand to hold.

'Thank you,' she said quietly. 'I might just do that.'

Had she been too hasty? Tessa pondered hours later when, having stayed on to do the overtime She owed after this morning's late start,' she walked slowly home. Lillian Foster might have been all dolled up in her finest, but to stand out as a shady character you didn't need to have horns and a tail!

Tessa knew nothing about her besides her name and where she was headed, and yet she'd invited her out for a drink as if they were old friends!

She shook her head impatiently,. as if trying to dislodge such unfounded thoughts. She'd always prided herself on being a good judge of character; after all, she had Esme pretty much sussed!

In Lillian Foster she'd seen an apprehension at landing in a new town with nowhere to go, and she'd been happy to help her. Might Victoria's similar fate have coloured her perception of the whole thing? She didn't think so, but no doubt time would tell.

It was strange, admittedly, that Lillian, a grown woman with a seemingly intelligent head on her shoulders, should take herself off to a new place without first having made arrangements where she would stay when she arrived, and to choose an industrial target like Birmingham! She'd been one of the few coming into the city when most were trampling her flat in their haste to leave it!

Perhaps she was running from something, or someone? Or perhaps she'd merely caught a train into Birmingham on an impulse and was at this moment up to nothing more untoward than making herself a nice cup of tea.

It was the society they were living in at the moment making her so easily and unnecessarily suspicious, Tessa thought bitterly, the palpable tension as the country seemed to be listening as one to the tick of an invisible clock. The current 'spot of bother' they were calling it on the wireless. Life as they knew it being catapulted upside down, more like.

Matthew, Bea and Victoria were gone, Leo was on tenterhooks waiting to receive his call-up papers, the factory and numerous other buildings were being piled high with sandbags, and when Tessa turned on a last minute whim to take her preferred stroll through the park rather than rush home to a house with yet another of her family missing, she was alarmed by the sight of armies of men with spades, hard at work digging up a once smooth carpet of green.

'Trenches, duck.' Noting her expression, the nearest man to her paused a moment to lean on his spade and mop a handkerchief across his brow. 'Not enough public shelters, see. Folk need somewhere to hide if we get bombed.'

The pungent scent of damp, freshly turned over soil filling her nostrils, Tessa made haste to tip him a nod and be on her way. As a family with a garden, they'd been told to expect their own shelter, one they'd have to construct it themselves, but it was just a matter of digging a big hole and securing it over the top.

'I'll not be going in no hole in the ground til the day they put me there in me coffin,' Esme had declared firmly, and knowing only too well the bother she'd have coaxing her out there, not least because Esme Lane had ventured no further than the outside privy for years now, Tessa didn't for one moment envy Hilary such a *task*.

Keen to leave a scene of such upheaval behind her, Tessa quickened her pace and was home within minutes.

She knew there was something wrong, something else, before she'd even walked through the door. In her armchair Esme was not, as was usual for this hour, dozing lightly, but sitting back against her cushion, sipping a cup of tea, and uncharacteristically quiet. Even Tessa's arrival which would normally raise a sarcastic observation or two was barely acknowledged.

At the table Hilary sat, with the old Singer sewing machine in front of her, running up the required blackout curtains Tessa had promised to make on her return, but when she opened her mouth to remind Hilary of this, the light from the gas lamp briefly illuminated the shine of tears spilling silently down her sister-in-law's cheeks, and Tessa knew that Hilary was sewing the curtains because she needed a distraction.

Sudden terror stealing her breath away, Tessa couldn't get the words out quickly enough.

'Matthew? ... Victoria?'

Hilary shook her head. 'Leo. He's gone.'

'Called up this morning,' Esme said

matter-of-factly. 'Knew it were just a matter of time, I did. Soon as he started playing soldiers, he were bound to be off sooner or later. Doing his duty, as well he should. Can't see the sense in blubbing over it ... '

The low whirr of the sewing machine ceased abruptly and Tessa turned to Hilary in time to see the look she gave Esme.

As far back as she could recall, Tessa had never known Hilary to stand up to her ma. A gentle chastising if Esme said or did something she feared might upset the applecart was the most Hilary would stretch to. Yet as the cold, hard bitterness in Hilary's eyes made her shiver, Tessa knew. that losing first her daughter and then her husband in one day, in Victoria's case in no small part due to Esme's interference, was starting to push Hilary further out of her ma's shadow than. she'd ever have thought to stray.

She'd not think of leaving Hilary the next day. With it being a Saturday, she wasn't expected at work, though Dorrie seemed to think Mr Ambrose, the owner, was thinking along the lines of adding Saturday mornings to the working week to keep on top of what he anticipated would be a constant demand for military uniforms, but as yet he'd made no such arrangements and Tessa's time was hers to spend as she always did.

The morning given over to helping Hillie clean through the house and do the washing, followed by a spot of lunch before she popped into the Black Horse for a drink with Bertie on her way into town where she liked to wander around the market stalls in the Bull Ring, on the lookout for cheap lace and ribbon, and the like.

★ ★ ★

A little of her usual quiet fortitude appearing to have trickled back after a good night's sleep, Hilary insisted Tessa had no need to change her plans on her account, but the dullness in her

56

eyes that were deeply ringed in shadow told a different tale. Hilary might have slept but 'good' was not the word Tessa would have used to describe the muffled sobbing she'd heard as she'd lain there, staring into the darkness, her own thoughts keeping her from drifting off until much later.

It was habit, instinct, that hauled Hilary up by the bootstraps. She'd carry on as normal, because she knew no other way to be, but inside her heart would be breaking. If for no other reason than to intercept any unfair comments from Esme, Tessa vowed that for today at least she'd remain at her sister-in-law's side.

Briefly she thought of Lillian Foster, who knew to find Tessa in the Black Horse at some point that afternoon, but chances are her second day in a new city would be a bit early for such frivolities. She'd only to ask Bertie, if she did happen to wander down there. He'd point her in the direction of Esme's house; knowing Bertie he'd probably walk her there himself.

When there was no sign of either of them, Tessa wasn't disappointed. For now Hillie needed her more.

With half its occupants missing, Esme's house seemed to echo with a sudden, almost eerie silence.

'Shows who made all the racket,' Esme muttered, and Tessa switched on the wireless that crackled into life with a burst of *Our Gracie*, momentarily doing its job of drowning out both Esme and the dreadful silence.

She switched it on again on Sunday morning, in time to hear the broadcast from Downing Street, the words that made her fear all over again for Victoria, for Bea, for her Matthew.

The waiting was over. The country was at war.

'That's that then,' Esme sighed. 'Got that pot on to boil, Hillie. I'm parched.'

A New Friend

As she fell into step with the caterpillar of women traipsing through the factory gates come Monday morning, Tessa felt reassured that this part of her life at least looked set to carry on as usual.

It was a little pocket of normality, if you overlooked the change in production from satin slips and cotton summer frocks to the coarse and scratchy serge of military tunics, not to mention a few hours' relief from Esme's caustic tones and the desolation in Hilary's eyes as she went about her chores with barely a word to say, not even to Tessa.

A fair few of the women around her looked even more bleary-eyed than usual, their pale faces witness to a first night of being unable to sleep for straining to hear the tell-tale drone of planes overhead.

She'd not fared much better herself, but it was not for her own safety she feared but for Matthew's, stuck on an air base in Norfolk, and for Victoria, wherever she may have landed.

The teachers from her school and others, travelling with the children, had known they were bound for Wales but beyond that could only promise to despatch details of specific towns or villages when they'd arrived and temporary addresses had been allocated. Until then the postman brought news of Victoria, Hilary's days were destined to be focussed on the long-awaited rattle of the letter box.

'We've a few minutes off first thing, Tess.' Dorrie Cooper's voice broke into her thoughts as she appeared beside her. 'Boss wants a word. Be about Saturday mornings, you'll see. Still, with the lads off fighting, suppose the least we can do is put in a bit of overtime to get 'em kitted out proper.'

'He'd be wise to take on a few extra staff while he's at it,' Tessa mused. 'Have you heard from Bea?'

Dorrie nodded, the usual pride in her

daughter's courage glowing in her eyes, but tempered now by fear for her safety.

'Letter arrived in last Friday's post.'

'She's all right?' Tessa faltered, when Dorrie paused.

'She's my Bea, smile on her face no matter what's asked of her. I'm just glad they're not sending women up in them planes ... oh, Tess, love, hark at me, going on, and with your Matthew off to get his wings ... I'm sorry, duck.'

Tessa shook her head quickly. She'd give short, sharp shrift to the likes of Esme at even the vaguest hint that Matthew was in danger, but Dorrie Cooper was a different kettle of fish.

'It's all right, Dorrie. He's ground crew just now so he'll not be going up, either.'

'We'll be thankful for that, then.' Dorrie squeezed Tessa's hand as, along with the rest of the women, they filed into the sewing room, where Mr Ambrose, the boss, was waiting to talk to them.

Dorrie's hunch had been spot on; in a matter of minutes Tessa found herself committed to spending Saturday mornings slaving away at her sewing machine.

They were none of them tied to the extra shift, Mr Ambrose had assured them; times like these there'd be plenty of folk looking for work who'd step in to pick up the shortfall, but he hoped those who were able would put their shoulders to the wheel ...

If Matthew could volunteer himself for the front line of duty, and Victoria could venture bravely to live with complete strangers, a few hours extra to her working week Tessa had no mind to grumble about.

Amidst the low hum of whispers that struck up like a symphony the moment the door closed after Mr Ambrose, she made her way to her machine, but again Dorrie appeared at her elbow.

'Tess, we've a new gel joining the ranks today, and as I hear you're already acquainted, might I ask you to show her the ropes?'

The young woman at Dorrie's side had swapped her fine coat and beret for the standard issue overalls and a head scarf, achieving a look so at odds with the elegantly dressed lady who'd rested a gloved hand on Tessa's arm three days earlier that it took her a moment to place her.

'Lillian Foster!'

'We meet again, Tessa Lane.' Lillian beamed at her. 'Seems you've a knack of coming to my rescue. One thing, mind. Call me Lil. Lillian makes me sound as if I should be tucked up in a rocking chair by the fire knitting tea cosies. Right then, you'd best teach me one end of a sewing machine from the other …'

Not for one moment had Tessa imagined that Lillian Foster might have come to Birmingham with the intention of slaving away at a sewing machine ten hours a day.

If she was to put down roots here she'd have to be wealthy indeed to get by with no job at all, but she seemed more suited to working in a smart boutique perhaps, or front of house in a high-class restaurant; at the very least her fine clothes had suggested she'd have time at her disposal to settle into her lodgings before she started knocking on factory doors.

Knowing Dorrie would be counting on her to have 'the new gel' up and running by the end of the shift, Tessa feared she'd have a task and a half on her hands, but despite Lil's cheerful claim to not know one end of a sewing machine from the other, she had a quick mind and by the time they broke for lunch, she and Tessa were able to work side by side.

'Your face this morning,' Lil chuckled when they were sitting in the canteen, eating their lunch. 'Right picture, it was.'

'Seeing you in overalls threw me for a minute.' Tessa smiled at her. 'Are you settled in at Mrs Cirelli's?'

'I'll say. Ginny Cirelli is a sweetheart. Falling over herself, she was to make sure I'd everything I needed. Did you know her husband came over here from Italy after the last war and he'd not been here a month when he proposed to her? Met on the bus, they did, and Ginny knew she'd found the man she wanted to marry before she reached her stop. Suppose there's no sense in waiting when you feel that strongly,' sighed Lil, who'd clearly struck up enough of a friendship with her landlady as to be on first name terms and sharing confidences.

She'd have needed a friendly ear though, with her being a stranger in town.

Recalling the relief that had flitted across Lil's face when she'd told her she could find her at the Black Horse of a Saturday afternoon, Tessa felt horribly guilty suddenly.

'Did you happen to drop by the Black Horse on Saturday?' she asked cautiously, and Lil's face creased into a smile.

'I'd not be here if I hadn't.' She twisted the stalk on her apple until it snapped off. 'Once he'd finished tinkling the ivories, I got talking to your pal, Bertie.'

'Thought as much.' Tessa smiled to herself. 'He's a bit of a charmer, is Bertie.'

'Indeed he is. Anyway, I happened to say as how I needed a job and he told me how his ma was after new girls for her line since half of them have joined up. Next thing I knew I were supping tea with Dorrie and, well, here I am.'

'All's well that's ended well then,' Tessa said quietly. 'I owe you an apology, mind. I was needed at home or I'd have been there as I said.'

Lil waved a hand dismissively. 'You've no need to apologise. Things crop up over which we've no control.' She lowered her voice. 'This Saturday morning's malarkey for one. Still, we've all got to do our bit, haven't we?'

'Might work out nicely, that,' Tessa pondered. 'Saturday morning shift, after which we drop by the Black Horse to catch a bit of Bertie's playlist ...'

'On our way into town?' Lil finished eagerly. 'I've a fancy for poking around the market hall — Ginny says there's a cafe does the best custard slices in the whole of Birmingham.'

'Green's Cafe,' Tessa supplied. 'Doughnuts aren't bad either.'

Lil beamed at her, taking it as set in

stone that they'd be spending Saturday afternoon browsing the stalls before retiring to Green's for something sugary and extravagant.

Tessa hadn't the heart to refuse her, and really, why should she? Weren't her Saturdays usually spent in this way? The browsing part at least — since Bea had joined up she'd not quite mastered the confidence needed for sitting in Green's by herself.

But it was the thought of Hilary that tweaked her collscience. Her afternoons she'd still be at liberty to spend as she always did the extra shift at the factory was a morning one and therefore impinged on the time she gave over to helping Hilary top and bottom the house. Should she make her excuses to Lil and abandon the chance to let her hair down after an even longer working week in favour of rushing home to scrub the back doorstep?

'Tessa?' Lil was watching her curiously. 'If you've other plans ...'

'Only involving a mop and bucket.

Nothing I can't leave til later.'

She'd do that, she decided. An afternoon in town with Lil, then back home to spend her evening catching up on the chores she'd tell Hilary to leave for her.

She'd need to impress upon her to do this because Hillie wasn't the type to sit around drinking tea when there were still steps to be scrubbed and grates to be black-leaded; under the present circumstances especially she'd leap at the chance of tackling the lot herself as a distraction from her fretting over Leo and Victoria; but Tessa wouldn't think ofleaving Hillie to do everything.

'We're on for Saturday then?' Lil prodded hopefully, and Tessa nodded, downing the dregs of her tea as the bell rang to summon them back to their machines.

'I'm looking forward to it.'

★ ★ ★

By the end of the first Saturday morning shift, Tessa felt more than ready for her afternoon with Lil. It had been a long week, and not due to the hours she put in at the factory — they were only days into the war and already the time she spent stitching army tunics was starting to feel like a blessed relief.

Was it only a matter of weeks since she'd felt cheered by the thought of a cup of tea and a chat with Hilary at the tail end of a long and arduous day at a sewing machine? Less than a month since Matthew's coat had hung on the hook by the door?

With her closest friend missing from her side for the first time since ... well, until now he'd always been there ... Tessa had at first found a little comfort in the presence of his sister, but Hilary was so preoccupied with worry for Leo and Victoria that a cup of tea and a chat with her did nothing to settle Tessa's mind. Her own worries about Matthew she'd instinctively looked to Hilary to ease, but instead they were compounded by her sister-in-law's constant fretting.

Within a day of each other, letters had

at last arrived from Leo and Victoria.

Brief but as detailed as he dared without falling foul of the censor's blue pencil, Leo's told of his current base somewhere in Lancashire.

'All these days she's spent in a lather waiting for the post to drop and all the time he's only been a matter o' miles away,' Esme said, shaking her head in disbelief. 'Near enough to pop home for his tea, he is.'

The same couldn't be said for Victoria, whose letter came from a remote village in the Welsh countryside, where she'd been billeted with a lady she called Granny Peg.

'Be right up her street it will, running wild with all them cows and horses and getting her frocks all mucky,' declared Esme, who didn't seem to be taking offence that her one and only grandchild had stumbled upon a replacement grandmother. 'Told you there'd be nowt to fret about, Hillie.

'There's your Leo with his feet firmly on British soil, instead of being shipped

70

off to foreign parts, and our Vic happy as a songbird up to her ears in country air. I'm sure I've no idea why you look like the bottom's dropped out of your world ... '

Tessa detected the slight tremble of apprehension in the old lady's tone and she knew that the subtle change in Hilary from dutiful daughter leaping to attention the second the kettle whistled, to distracted wife and mother with her thoughts very definitely elsewhere had not gone urmoticed by Esme.

Come Saturday, Tessa was just grateful to have something else to think about for a while. Not that she could ever forget what was happening around them. As Lil threaded her arm through Tessa's and the pair of them strode out through the factory gates and on towards the Black Horse, to all sides of them were signs of war, from the anti-blast tape secured across shop windows to the all too frequent crunch of glass underfoot where a car had come a cropper in the blackout.

One thing she'd say for Brum folk though, they'd enough spirit to be up and about their business no matter what changes a week into war was already starting to bring. A fair few of them seemed to be packed into the Black Horse, all gathered together for a bit of a sing-song.

'Quite the local hero, that Bertie,' Lil noticed, when she and Tessa had fought their way to a table in the corner. 'Reckon half of Brum's gathered round that piano.'

'He has made a bit of a name for himself,' Tessa agreed. 'Can't be many round here haven't heard him play.'

As Bertie struck up the opening bars of a popular swing number, Lil leaned in closer to make herself heard above the rousing chorus of voices that accompanied him.

'Knows his way round a piano, I'll say that for him. Why's he not off in the army or flying planes like the rest of them?'

'Bertie works for the Gas Board,' Tessa explained. 'Reserved occupation.

He's not been called up.'

She glanced across at Bertie, who smiled and tipped her a wink between songs. He'd protested indignation that his job was on the reserved list, she remembered. He'd claimed to be frustrated that he'd not have the opportunity to enlist and fight for his country.

But she was being unfair. Wasn't Bertie one of her oldest and dearest friends?

She just wished Matthew's fate hadn't been so very different. But he'd been so determined to enrol in the air force that he'd have gone anyway, and now he was on an air base in Norfolk, risking life and limb, while she was sitting in the Black Horse, listening to Bertie belt out a string of cheery little numbers and planning a carefree afternoon of wandering around the market hall with Lil.

Instinctively Tessa closed her right hand over the gold band on her left, as if the cold metal pressing into her palm was a way of holding onto Matthew, of keeping him safe.

When she saw the ever-sharp Lil's eyes

on her, she braced herself for the subject she'd yet to tackle.

Over the past week she and Lil had chatted constantly as they worked side by side. With the other women at the factory Tessa pleasantly passed the time of day, as she tended to do with most folk she met, but not even with Bea had she talked so endlessly over the whirr of the sewing machines.

Lil reminded her of a sparrow, chattering away to her heart's content. Swept along with her boundless enthusiasm for everything from Ginny Cirelli's home cooking to the crackly records that played on the gramophone Mr Ambrose permitted to raise the women's spirits, there had been odd moments over the past week when Tessa had almost forgotten there was a war on.

They'd talked of everything but the ring on Tessa's finger, and the man who'd put it there. After a week in close quarters, Lil would surely have noticed the thin gold band and recognised it for what it was, but she'd not enquired about Matthew, and until she was sure her new friend would understand, Tessa had kept it to herself.

But now Lil's eyes travelled to Tessa's hand where she was twisting her ring nervously.

'Reckon it's high time you told me about your Matthew.'

Tessa blinked in surprise. When had she so much as mentioned Matthew's name? But when the jaunty melody from the piano ceased and Bertie announced he'd be taking a short break before sauntering over to their table, the penny dropped.

Of course, Bertie would have been talking! This time last week, on finding a pretty girl hanging on his every word, and discovering they'd a mutual acquaintance in Tessa, he'd have had a fair bit to say for himself.

That'd be why Lil had held back from asking about Tessa's ring, when it must have been conspicuous as the only subject they'd not covered; knowing that Tessa would be missing Matthew as she'd miss her right arm, Bertie would have warned Lil to let her talk about him in her own time.

She'd have taken offence at the ease with which he'd discussed her business with Lil when as yet she'd been little more than a stranger, had he been anyone other than Bertie Cooper.

'Blow me down, if it's not the new Mrs Lane!' Bertie grinned at her as he slid into a chair opposite. 'Thought you might have swapped sing songs round the piano for knitting by the fire now you're a respectable married woman?'

'About as likely as you keeping anything to yourself for more than five minutes, that is,' Tessa retorted. 'Tell me, Bertram, do the rest of Brum know I've a ring on my finger or do I need to take out an advert in the Birmingham Post?'

'Blimey, Tess. Mrs Lane in name and nature — you'd best watch it or you'll be turning into Esme.' Bertie winked at her before transferring his attention to Lil. 'The lovely Miss Foster. We meet again.

Any chance you've time for another drink?'

With Bertie waylaid at the bar by the usual barrage of song requests, Lil turned to Tessa, her expression suddenly grave.

'You've no need to tell me about Matthew if you'd rather keep it to yourself, Tess.'

'No, it's all right.' Tessa smiled reassuringly at her. 'There's not much to tell though.'

Suddenly she found she wanted to talk about Matthew. At home she'd taken to keeping off the subject for fear of stirring Hilary up to further fretting, and to steer clear of more scathing comments from Esme that *her Mattie* was messing about on the ground when he'd signed up to fly them planes.

It would be nice to be able to talk about him with Lil. To bring him back into the conversation as if he'd never left it She'd no need to explain the particular circumstances surrounding their wedding day — just to tell Lil about him would be enough — that's if Bertie hadn't explained it already.

'Bertie said you and Matthew have been friends since you were babbies,' Lil prompted, and Tessa smiled fondly.

'The best of friends. We grew up together, see. There's not been a day we've not talked … until now.'

'You must miss him,' Lil said gently. 'He's in the RAF, Bertie was telling me … '

'What else did Bertie tell you?' Tessa shook her head in silent exasperation.

All this fretting about how much to confide in Lil when courtesy of Bertie she clearly knew — the whole story, chapter and verse! 'Suppose you know Matthew and I weren't walking out together? That he only married me to keep me under his ma's roof?'

Barely had the words left her mouth when Lil's eyes widened in surprise.

'I didn't … but I do now.'

Tessa stared at her. 'You mean … Bertie didn't say … '

'Not a dickie-bird,' Lil assured her.

'Way he told it was that you and Matthew got married for the oldest reason in the book.' She smiled at Tessa's perplexed expression. 'Love, Tess.'

'He knows that's not how it was,' Tessa murmured, watching Bertie balance a tray of drinks as he weaved his way back towards their table, amidst the goodnatured jostling of an audience eager for his musical repertoire to resume.

'I've no chance of a drink in peace with this lot clamouring for a sing-song.'

He set the tray down, his eyes sparkling. 'Best get back to the old piano. Up for a chorus or two, Tess? Drag that there Lil out of her corner — couldn't get her to join in for love nor money last week!'

'Your famous charm wearing thin, is it, Bertie?' Tessa managed a smile as she waved him away back to his piano and his adoring public. There was no point getting herself into a dither because he'd been telling tales about her and Matthew.

Of everyone she knew, Bertie Cooper could be relied on the most to tell it as he saw it and no messing, but on this occasion he'd been her friend first and foremost. He'd have edited the truth to save her from having to answer any awkward questions, and to no avail because she'd gone and blurted it all out herself.

She turned to Lil, who was sipping her drink quietly, a wistful look in her eyes as she watched the many people crowded around the piano, singing their hearts out.

A stranger in town, she'd have perhaps been too shy to join in last week — though the Lillian Foster Tessa knew was anything but bashful!

'We'll join Bertie for a song or two then, shall we? Before we go?' It was a rhetorical question. Not needing to wait for an answer from Lil, Tessa was up and halfway round the table before she realised her friend hadn't moved.

'Lil?'

'You go on,' she said firmly. 'I'm all right here.'

'You don't like singing?'

Tessa knew she'd not imagined the look in Lil's eyes a moment earlier as she'd watched the crowd clustered around Bertie and his piano. It was the look of a child with her nose pressed up against the glass of a sweet shop window.

But Lil shook her head slowly. 'I've no voice for singing.'

'Nor have most of this lot,' Tessa ventured. 'Hark at them.'

'I can't sing,' Lil persisted stiffly. 'So I don't sing.'

A recent memory drifted into focus as Tessa faltered halfway between their table and the piano, torn between her loyalty to Bertie and her consideration for Lil.

She and Lil, toiling away side by side in the factory, their feet working the pedals of the sewing machines in time to the rhythm of the music that crackled into life from Mr Ambrose's old gramophone, the involuntary humming from Lil, the spontaneity with which she'd broken into song, albeit quietly and very much to herself, but Tessa had spent enough time with Bertie and his army of devoted followers to know one thing for certain — amongst them Lillian Foster's singing would stand out as the voice of an angel.

But Tessa knew instinctively she'd have no luck persuading Lil to join her and the others at the piano with Bertie. She knew too that Lil would have her reasons, same as Tessa had her reasons for wanting to keep the truth about her and Matthew to herself.

Her mind made up, she retraced her steps to the table. 'Bertie has enough admirers. He'll not notice if I'm there or not. Come on, we've stalls to explore and cakes to demolish.'

Gratefully, Lil threaded her arm back through Tessa's, her usual good humour already on the way to being restored. As they passed the piano, Bertie did indeed notice them, but instead of fixing Tessa with a silent admonishment for slinking off, his gaze rested fleetingly on Lil before he turned his attention back to the keys.

'Crikey!' Lil exclaimed, tightening her hold on Tessa's arm as they were forced to push their way amongst the throng of shoppers filling every inch of the Bull Ring. 'Is it always this busy?'

'Saturday afternoons,' Tessa commented wryly. 'Reckon half of Brum must have pay burning a hole in their pocket.'

Wandering round the market hall, their senses were assailed by the richly sweet scent of stalls laden with fruit, the gaudily painted crockery stacked up on another, and the cheerful, piercing tones of traders shouting their wares. Tessa paused at the haberdashery stall, as she did every week, to peruse the selection of lace, ribbons, buttons and the like.

'All right then, duck?' The plump, middle aged woman who ran the stall grinned at one of her most loyal customers. 'Missed yer last week, I did.'

'I'd things to see to at home, Mary,' Tessa told her briefly, her attention on the thick, gauzy crepe-de-chine she stroked between her fingers.

'Where'd you find this?'

'Chovey shop round back of the station,' Mary announced proudly. 'Some right nice pieces if you've the time to look proper.' She eyed Tessa hopefully.

'Make someone a smashing blouse, would that.'

'Three or four petticoat slips, I was thinking,' Tessa pondered.

'Grand idea. Two shillings to you, Tess.'

'Come off it, Mary.' Tessa turned the fabric over in her hand, pointing out the soiled patch Mary had folded in such a way as to hide it from the unsuspecting customer. 'Way that's stained, you can't have paid much above a shilling for it'

She was aware of Lil beside her, watching this exchange in a stunned silence. In her world she'd not have had much cause to barter.

Mary Shook her head in disbelief. 'I've yet to get one over on you, gel. One and sixpence suit you better?'

'Throw in half a dozen of them pearl buttons and you've got yourself a sale,'

Tessa told her firmly, and less than a moment later she'd handed over her money and moved off with her purchases in a paper bag, a stunned Lil at her side.

'Blimey, Tess,' Lil exclaimed, when they were sat upstairs in Green's with a cup of tea and a custard slice. 'That poor woman ...'

'Mary's no poor woman,' Tessa assured her. 'She's pleasant enough but she'll push her luck if she thinks she's half a chance of getting away with it.'

'Met her match with you though.' Lil looked at her with a new respect.

'I'd no idea you were so into this sewing lark. Not just a day job, then?'

Tessa shook her head. 'Been making my own clothes since I got to grips with Esme's archaic sewing machine.' She smiled to herself as she stirred sugar into her tea. 'I patch, I darn, I mend everything til it's fit for nothing but the rag bag.'

'Well, I never.' Lil sunk a fork into her custard slice, oozing yellow all over the pristine white plate. 'Did you make your wedding dress?'

Tessa glanced up at her, taken aback for a moment. She'd assumed her outburst at the Black Horse earlier had drawn a line under the subject of Matthew and their wedding. Lil had seemed to know to leave it be, same as Tessa had known not to push her into singing with Bertie and the others. But Lil laid her fork down, all her attention on Tessa as she waited to hear about a subject that obviously held her captivated.

It was her dressmaking skills more than her marriage to Matthew that had sparked Lil's interest, Tessa thought.

'I did, but it started life as a simple summer frock,' she explained. 'Made from an old cotton tablecloth. I just stitched some cream lace frill round the hem and the neckline, and I had myself a perfectly acceptable wedding dress.'

'Talent like that, you've no business to be slaving away at Ambrose's,' Lil declared, a twinkle in her eye. 'Taking up a wage some poor untalented soul such as the likes of me would be glad of.'

Tessa raised an eyebrow at her. 'And what, pray tell, am I supposed to do instead?'

'Set yourself up as a professional dressmaker,' Lil replied simply, as if it was that easy. With some difficulty Tessa resisted the temptation to point out the disparity between her world and the one Lil had certainly once inhabited, even if she'd since come down to earth with a bump.

'That would take capital I don't have,' she explained. 'I'd need to find suitable premises, for which I'd have to pay a month or two's rent upfront, not to mention the cost of bulk buying materials — cotton, silks, taffeta, muslin — I'd need ample stock of fringe, braid, buttons, ribbons ...'

'Not that you've given it more than a passing thought.' Lil grinned at her. 'Tess, you've clearly got a passion for it.'

Tessa smiled at her own exuberance. 'Hark at me, going on like a child in a toy shop.'

'So you've thought about it?' Lil persisted.

'Once or twice,' Tessa admitted, idly swirling her fork around to make patterns in the custard 'It's just a dream, Lil. Least I get to make up and sew my own designs, even if they are only just for me and people I know.' She chuckled softly. 'Anyone's guess how long that old Singer machine of Esme's will hold out, mind.'

'You've a marriage allowance from the RAF?' Lil enquired, and when Tessa nodded, 'Save it up towards a new machine.'

If only she were free to do just that! 'It goes in the family pot. We're missing Matthew's wage, see. With Leo off as well, what Hilary gets from the anny, that goes straight in too. We've two less mouths to feed, three with Victoria evacuated, but even so it's a stretch.'

Lil nodded sympathetically. 'What did Matthew do in peacetime?'

'Bus driver. Knows the streets of Brum like the back of his hand.'

'Not a reserved occupation then like Bertie?'

Tessa's heart twisted painfully but she forced a smile. 'No, but it wouldn't have made any difference ifit was. He'd still have gone.'

'Something to prove?' Lil guessed. 'Or was he just after flying one of them Spitfires?'

She'd be trying to lighten the mood, Tessa knew that, but when it came to Matthew she'd not be jollied out of anything. She missed him, worried about him and it all hurt too much to be flippant.

'His pa died because of the Great War,' she said stiffly. 'Mustard gas in his chest, it was a ticking clock after that. Matthew's set on doing his bit to win this war so Arthur didn't die for nothing.'

Lil placed a hand over Tessa's. 'Not much comfort, though, is it? When you miss him like you'd miss your right arm?'

Tessa looked up at her sharply. 'Who said I ... oh, of course. I was forgetting.

Bertie's been talking.'

But Lil shook her head solemnly. 'Bertie said nothing of the sort.' She smiled as she dug her fork once more into her custard slice. 'He'd no need to. I've got eyes, you know, Tess.'

Tessa knew what she was implying, that there was more to her and Matthew than she'd yet confessed to, a seed of suspicion in all likelihood sown by Bertie, however well-meant his motives, and in spite of Lil's protestations to the contrary.

She'd have put her right, explain the reasons Matthew had for making her his wife, were it not for one pair of shoes Lil had so unwittingly filled. Pushing her to acknowledge her dream of being a dressmaker and refusing to believe there was no more to her and Matthew than met the eye, Lil was precious to Tessa for one very good reason.

She reminded her of Bea.

Together Again

Birmingham was held fast in the grip of a freezing winter as Christmas approaches. With the nights drawing-in, and with them a bitter cold that clouded her breath in front of her, Tessa was no longer quite so inclined to dilly dally as she made her way home each evening through the thick, cloying blanket of darkness that was the blackout.

For a month or two now folk had been allowed to carry torches, provided the beam was dimmed with tissue paper and aimed nowhere else but at their feet.

Tessa carried her torch with her but it made so little difference she'd long since switched it off. In this city she knew her way around, even in complete darkness.

Not so much the case for Lil. She'd a sharp enough mind so that routes she took regularly, such as the walk from the factory back to Ginny Cirelli's boarding house, she quickly grew familiar with, but left to negotiate her way home from town, or the Black Horse, she was reluctant as yet to attempt such an expedition without either Tessa or Bertie, or both, by her side.

Ever the chivalrous gentleman, Bertie was only too pleased to escort Lil wherever she needed to go.

'Only right I should be walking you home anyway,' he told her. 'Even if the city were lit up like a Christmas tree.' Turning to Tessa, he added, 'You too, Mrs Lane. I won't half get it from Matthew if I don't see you safely back under Esme's roof.'

'Give over, Bertie,' Tessa sighed. 'Matthew knows I don't need looking after.'

'I'm walking you home, Tess,' he persisted, a twinkle in his eye as he grinned at her. 'If you've summat to say about it, take it up with your other half. Me, I'm just the messenger boy.'

So Matthew had told Bertie to look out for her? Of course he had! He knew Tessa was no meek and feeble slip of a thing who needed a hand in hers before she'd even cross the street; if anyone knew Tessa was more than capable of fighting her own way through life it was Matthew; but nonetheless he wanted to see her safe, it was the very reason he'd married her, and if he couldn't be there with her, it fell to Bertie to make sure no harm came to her.

She'd be the same, Tessa thought, if the boot were on the other foot.

If only Bea were stationed at West Raynham with Matthew instead of a few miles away at Coltishall, she'd be relying on her to watch over him. As far as she could, Bea did so anyway, easing Tessa's mind considerably when one of her all too infrequent letters mentioned a dance they'd both attended. It didn't matter that Matthew had danced with Bea; all Tessa cared about was that he was still safe and well, and able to dance at all.

He'd every right to nights off from having to think about the war, as did Tessa, Lil and Bertie, and the others who crowded into the Black Horse of an evening until it was packed to bursting.

Try as he might, and disregarding every one of Tessa's warnings to leave her be, Bertie had yet to persuade Lil to get up and sing with him, but the haste with which she'd fled the inn on that first Saturday they'd not seen since. Lil would not be cajoled into singing a note, but it was the company she treasured.

She and Tessa were firm friends, and Bertie had clearly taken a bit of a shine to Lillian Foster. As yet they'd not started walking out together, but Tessa knew Lil found the irrepressible Bertie absolutely delightful. She was sharp, perceptive, and more than a match for his quick wit.

'There goes the future Mrs Cooper,' Bertie was fond of declaring, albeit when Lil was out of earshot, but as likely as it did seem that Lil was developing a soft spot for Bertie, she'd yet to confess as much and Tessa thought enough of him that she had to at least warn him that his hopes may be dashed.

'Bertie, for all you know Lil just thinks of you as the daft chap who makes her laugh and walks her home.'

'That's how you think of me, Tess,' Bertie corrected her. 'Knight in shining armour with a piano and a torch — until Matthew shows his face again, at any rate.' He smiled knowingly. 'It's not how it were meant to be, you know. You and me, Bea and Matthew — would have worked out nicely, that.'

Tessa blinked in surprise. 'Bertie, you're a treasure, but ... '

'You've no need to fret, Tess.' He chuckled softly. 'Lil's the light o' my life. Just wish she'd get up and sing with me.'

'She's shy of having an audience, perhaps,' Tessa pondered, and Bertie's face was a picture of disbelief as he caught at her sleeve, drawing her to one side so he could talk unheard by anyone else.

'Soon as I met her I thought she had a look of someone, but it took me a while ...' He paused to watch Lil laughing with the barmaid as she paid for their drinks. 'You know who her ma is, Tess?'

'She's never mentioned her.' Over a

cream doughnut in Green's Cafe Lil had eventually confided in Tessa that she'd been living in a village in the remote Welsh countryside with her grandmother, Margaret, but she'd come to the city to do her bit for the war effort.

Beyond that, details had been sketchy but Tessa had got the distinct impression from Lil that this was because there was simply not much else to tell.

In any case, she'd certainly never mentioned a mother.

'Marianne Foster,' Bertie whispered, shaking his head in disbelief at Tessa's blank expression. 'You've not heard of her? She's a big name in the music world — wasn't that long ago she was singing in all the revues and music halls down London's West End. Voice of an angel, she has. Not heard much of her for a while, mind.'

'Maybe she's off digging spuds instead,' Tessa said. 'Chipping in with the rest of us mere mortals.' She turned to watch Lil thoughtfully. 'I'm not convinced, Bertie. She'd have told me if her ma were as famous as all that ... wouldn't she?'

He shrugged. 'For all we know, they might have had a falling out. Can't argue with genetics, mind. If she's Mari-anne Foster's daughter, there's no doubt about it — she'll have a cracking voice on her.'

'You might have this all wrong,' Tessa warned him, as Lil began threading her way back towards them, but Bertie shook his head firmly.

'She's the spit of her, Tess. I've not got it wrong.'

'Leave her to tell us in her own time, then, and I do hope you're not. after courting her just to advance your con-tacts in the music business, Bertram Cooper.'

Bertie looked hurt. 'There's some who would, but I'm not one of them. Tess, it took me weeks to figure out whose daughter she is, but only days to know I'd found the woman I'm to spend the rest of my life with, even if I'm never to pass the time of day with her ma and even if Lil herself never sings a note.'

He grinned ruefully. 'Be smashing if she did, though.'

She'd been unfair, Tessa chided herself. Bertie wasn't the type to have a hidden agenda. If he had one at all, it didn't stay hidden for long! His heart he wore very visibly on his sleeve.

Lil would have to be looking the other way every time they were together to remain unaware of it, but though she hadn't said as much, as Christmas drew closer Tessa got the distinct impression her friend was growing as enamoured with Bertie's company as he was with hers.

The up side for Tessa was that she found it much easier to slip away and walk home by herself unchallenged.

She was finding too that she was almost relieved to be free of their company.

As fond as she was of them both, she was starting to feel very much the gooseberry. Neither of them would have intended her to feel that way, she knew.

She'd only to say something ... but she'd no intention of doing so.

Bertie was the happiest she'd ever seen him, and Lil seemed the most at ease she'd been since stepping off the train on her first day in Binningham. If she was the daughter of Marianne Foster, and Bertie would not be convinced otherwise, she'd yet to mention her. Given Lil's normal tendency to chatter ten to the dozen about everything, Tessa suspected that the subject of her mother for whatever reason might be too difficult or painful to bring up.

Talking and laughing with Bertie, chances are she never gave it a passing thought.

Only too aware of how it felt to belong to a mother who meant nothing to her but a lasting emptiness and a guilt she'd hardly dared question, not even with Matthew to hold her hand, Tessa was happy to leave Lil and Bertie in peace.

Under normal circumstances she'd perhaps not have felt as excluded as she did. If the country wasn't at war, Matthew would be home, and there by her side like he'd always been, instead of

whirling Bea around a dance hall somewhere in the wilds of Norfolk.

Not for one moment did Tessa suspect them of anything; she and Matthew
might not have married for love but she
knew he'd never betray her; it was more
the fact that he and Bea were occasional
company for each other, as on a far more
regular basis were Lil and Bertie, while
Tessa was left feeling very much alone.

It was daft, of course it was. There
wasn't one of the four of them who
didn't think the world of her, as she did
of them. It was just how much she was
missing Matthew that made her feel at
odds with everything else too.

He'd written to tell her he'd be home
for Christmas. A week they'd given him,
the first time he'd had since joining up
four months ago. As she trudged home
each night in the deepening snow that
numbed her feet and left her face raw
with cold, Tessa was counting the days
until she had her Matthew back where
he belonged, for however brief a time.

Hilary had written to Granny Peg

in Wales to request Victoria home for Christmas, and received a reply promising she'd be duly despatched. With Leo due for a week's leave, too, it seemed to Tessa as if her sister-in-law suddenly sprang back to life.

Weeks she'd spent dragging herself listlessly from one thankless chore to another, but knowing she'd see her husband and her daughter in a matter of days perked Hilary up no end.

Watching her flit around the house, singing under her breath as she hadn't done in so long, Tessa's own spirits were lightened in turn, but nevertheless she couldn't help fearing how much harder Hillie would fall once Christmas was over and she was forced to wave Leo and Victoria off for a second time.

Not that it would be any easier for Tessa when Matthew returned to West Raynham, the thought of which she shied away from instinctively. For now there was no sense fretting about it. They'd have a whole week together first. She couldn't, and didn't want, to think

101

beyond that. She didn't blame Hilary for being the same.

★ ★ ★

Victoria arrived home the day before Christmas Eve, with both Leo and Matthew expected within hours of each other the following morning.

Bertie had been booked to play at the Black Horse that evening, for a good old seasonal knees-up, as he described it, to which Tessa had promised she'd accompany Lil. She'd not seen her niece for four months but Victoria's first hours back under Esme's roof it was only fair she spent exclusively with Hilary. Esme would of course be dozing in her chair by the fire but provided they were quiet, for the most part they'd be left to chat together, just the two of them.

Tessa smiled to herself as she walked dovm the side of the house, an image in her mind that warmed her heart of the scene she'd left behind her.

Hilary and Victoria, cuddled together

like two little mice, whispering in the firelight so as not to wake Granny.

Making her way through the unlit streets of Birmingham with as much confidence as she'd stroll along the same route in broad daylight, Tessa arrived at the Black Horse in good time to find Lil, who had naturally been escorted there by Bertie himself, halfway up a ladder helping to string up paper chains.

She'd certainly slotted into place as a native Brummagem lass, Tessa thought as she watched Lil bounce back down the ladder, and heads together with Jeannie, the landlady, survey the finished decorations.

'Tessa!' Lil beamed at her. 'You've made it then!'

'I promised you I would,' Tessa reminded her, but Lil narrowed her eyebrows to look at her pointedly.

'Isn't Matthew due in the morning?'

'Yes, which is all the more reason for me to spend the evening here with you. Sitting at home listening to the clock ticking I'd be going slowly bananas.'

With the stalwart spirit shared by Binningham folk everywhere, the Black Horse was packed even tighter than usual as so many. were determined to enjoy Christmas despite the lurking shadow of war, but Tessa and Lil managed to squeeze their way to their usual table in the corner.

'Dorrie's invited me for Christmas day,' Lil revealed, her cheeks a little pinker as she smiled at Tessa. 'Bea's due back tomorrow, Bertie says. Be nice to be part of their Christmas.'

'Bertie would have it no other way,' Tessa told her. 'You know you'd be welcome to come to us instead, but I've a notion you'd prefer to spend the day with Mr Musical Maestro over there.'

Lil's smile widened. 'He's smashing, Tess, he really is, and Dorrie treats me like her own daughter.'

Now was not the time to ask after Bertie's suspicions that Lil already had a mother, Tessa thought wryly, though there was one question she felt able to ask.

'What of your grandmother? You've no plans to visit her over Christmas then?'

The smile faded as Lil shook her head quickly. 'My life is here now,' she said stiffly. 'With Bertie and Dorrie, and you, Tess. I've decent lodgings, a fairly paid job and friends I treasure. Nothing to go back to Wales for.'

Tessa patted her hand. 'I'm sorry, Lil I didn't mean anything by it.'

'Only hours before Matthew gets here then,' Lil declared brightly, seizing on a change of subject. 'You'll be meeting him off the train, I take it?'

She'd have in mind a hearts and flowers reunion, Tessa knew, but though it would be nothing of the sort, the sentiment behind it was close enough that she felt no need to enlighten her.

The love she and Matthew had wasn't how Lil suspected it to be, but it was love all the same.

She loved him as her best friend in the world and if Lil envisaged a poignant moment when Tessa would fly into Matthew's arms, she'd not be far wrong.

'Will I have the pleasure of making his acquaintance or are you keeping him to yourself?' Lil enquired, her head cocked to one side like an inquisitive little sparrow.

Tessa smiled as she shook her head. 'I've a feeling your paths will cross at some point. He'll be wanting to catch up with Bertie, see.'

In the few moments she'd been chatting with Tessa, Lil's eyes had never strayed far from the piano, where Bertie was leading a room full of revellers in a hearty rendition of a Christmas classic.

Now she rested her gaze on him as he paused between songs to retrieve his glass from the top of the piano.

Briefly his eyes met Lil's and Tessa caught the look that passed between them.

'Thinks the world of you, our Bertie does,' she ventured. 'Reckon you mean more to him than his precious piano, and I've not had cause to say that before.'

Lil smiled wistfully. 'Make his day, wouldn't it, if I were to sidle up to that piano and sing my heart out with the rest of them.'

'It makes his day that you're-here at all,' Tessa told her gently. 'Makes no odds to Bertie if you never sing a note ... '

Depositing her empty glass onto the table with a thump, Lil got to her feet, a steely determination glinting in her eyes as she crossed the room to the piano where Bertie, on seeing her approach, dispersed the crowd clustered around him to make room for her.

Following at a more sedate pace, Tessa saw Lil lean in to whisper into Bertie's ear and he began to play once more, but this time with Lil beside him, her hand resting on his shoulder as the angelic voice that was her genetic legacy filled the room and stunned the rest of the crowd into an awestruck silence.

She'd no need to stay much longer after that. Lil and Bertie were united in their efforts to lead the crowd in a heart-felt refrain, and once they'd got over their amazement at discovering their own lit-tle starlet amongst them, there wasn't a voice in the whole of the inn not raised once more in time with hers. Tessa knew there was little chance her friends would notice she'd slipped out into the night.

A thick curtain of snowflakes drifted gracefully down around her as she began a slow walk back to Esme's house.

She'd had in mind the whole evening spent in the Black Horse, joining in with the festivities with Lil and Bertie and the rest; she'd not planned on leaving quite so soon. But it was late enough already that Victoria would surely be in bed when she returned and she'd not have intruded on Hilary's evening catching up with her daughter.

To err on the side of caution she could have stayed on at the inn for a little longer, but she'd felt alone, and restless, as if there was nowhere she really needed to be, and no-one who needed her to be with them.

Silly to sink into such low spirits when Matthew was due back in the morning, Tessa chided herself. She paused for a minute to look up at the night sky, raising a hand to shield her eyes from eddies of snow that swirled straight at her. The moon was full and a beacon lighting the way through the blackout — the snow itself illuminating the streets far more effectively than the diluted beam of a pocket torch.

Sudden fear gripped her. What if the snow delayed Matthew's return? What if the trains from Norfolk failed to run at all?

She shook her head impatiently as she started walking once more.

She couldn't think like that. Matthew was coming home. She'd be seeing him in a few hours, snow or no snow.

With the streets around her deserted, her own footsteps seemed to echo in the darkness. Hers ... and someone else's,

She was being followed. Never had she been afraid to walk alone in the blackout but now panic gripped her as her fingers clenched around the torch in her pocket, groping for the switch ... she'd shine it right at him, whoever he was, blind him for long enough that she could make a run for it ...

But there was something familiar about the figure looming out of the shadows that stilled her hand.

'Tess, it's me.'

'Matthew?'

He was a little thinner, and his hair was cut shorter, but he was still Matthew — she'd have known him among hundreds.

'Hello, wife.' He grinned at her, dropping his kitbag down into the snow so he had both arms free to close tightly around her when she flew into them.

'I've missed you too much,' Tessa told him softly. 'Why'd you not tell me you were getting here tonight? I'd have been there to meet you off the train if I'd known.'

Matthew's eyes sparkled. 'I can go back if you like? Meet you as promised in the morning?'

'Don't you dare.'

'Ah well, can't say as I've much of a fancy for kipping outside in the snow, so home with you it is.'

Brushing off the worst of the snow from his kitbag, Matthew shouldered it once more before taking Tessa's arm in his.

'Snowing a blizzard down in Norfolk,' he explained as they walked the short distance to Esme's house. 'Bad enough that it might stop the trains, so they let us go a bit earlier. I'd no chance to let you know, Tess, I'm sorry.'

Recalling her fear of only moments before that the snow would keep Matthew stranded and she'd not get to see him at all, Tessa tightened her hold on his arm.

'You're here safely. That's all that matters.'

'Took long enough though,' he sighed. 'Snow's starting to settle on the tracks already, see. Trains were crawling along. I should have got into Brum hours ago. Victoria get home all right?'

'Back with Hillie as of this morning. Leo's not due til tomorrow, though.'

She glanced up at the sky thick with yet more snow. 'It'll break her heart if he

111

can't get here.'

'The Leo I know will walk the whole way rather than not see her,' Matthew murmured. 'If I had to I'd have done the same myself.'

Tessa rested her head against his shoulder as they trudged past a row of shops, their windows blacked out and looking grim and desolate.

'What about Bea? She's not due yet either.'

'Home safe and sound,' Matthew assured her. 'She caught the same train as me, so I walked her back to her ma's, rather than have her traipsing the streets on her own at this hour ... ' He broke off suddenly, and taking a firmer hold on Tessa's arm, drew her into the narrow alley between the butchers and the post office, over which the roofs of both extended far enough that for a riioment they were sheltered from the snow.

'Well, there's no Esme to talk your ear off, granted, but I'd prefer a cup of tea and a sit by the fire to lurking here and getting frostbite.' Tessa smiled at him, but Matthew's expression was grave.

'I've things I need to say to you without Ma putting her two-penceworth in.'

He looked her up and down. 'Where've you been, all dolled up like that?'

Tessa could feel herself frowning at him as she replied stiffly. 'Black Horse. Bertie' s playing tonight.'

'Of course he is. There's none like our Bertie for cheering the mood.'

Anger glinted in Matthew's eyes. 'Pity he's not so good at keeping his word.'

'I don't need a chaperone, Matthew,' Tessa said quietly.

'That'll be why you nearly jumped clean out of your skin when you heard me behind you then.' He stared pointedly at her. 'I don't want you out at this hour.'

'You've no say in what I do.' With a steely resolve that matched his, Tessa faced him stubbornly.

'You're my wife, Tess,'

'Mrs Lane in name only,' she retorted. 'I'll not be doing as Esme did, Matthew.

Years of running round after your pa, no wonder she's flaked out in that old arm-chair. You'll have no luck tying me to the kitchen sink, ring or no ring ... '

'Have you finished?' He snatched her left hand in his, pulling her glove off to reveal the gold band sitting snugly on her finger. 'See this, Tess? Why'd you think I put it there?'

'Best way you could think of to keep me here and tied to your ma's apron strings.' But the stricken look on his face made her soften a little. 'I know why. You did it to keep me from being called up.'

'Well then,' he said flatly. 'Twenty-one years, Tess. You'll not stop me fretting now.' Holding her hand in his, he pulled her glove back on. 'Come on, we'd best get home before we freeze.'

She couldn't be cross with him for wanting her kept safe, Tessa told herself as arm in arm they walked the rest of the way. For her part hadn't she wished so many times she'd lost count that Bea were stationed nearer to Matthew for that very purpose?

They'd at least managed to catch the same train back from Norfolk. Good job too, by the sounds of it. If they'd waited any longer, chances are there'd have been no trains to catch. But they'd both made it back home safe and in one piece, after a journey so slow and tedious they'd have been invaluable company for each other.

She could just picture the relief on their faces when at last they'd stepped out onto Birmingham soil, Bea's eyes that were as bright as a squirrel's shining with happiness as she linked her arm through Matthew's for the walk back to Dorrie's house, the pair of them so pleased to be home that they'd have been laughing and joking together the whole way ...

Tessa leaned into him, so tired suddenly she felt like she'd been awake for four months.

Was she really cross because Bea, her dear friend Bea, had needed to be seen safely home?

She was just feeling a bit out of sorts.

For four long months she'd missed Matthew every day. Sixteen weeks of talking about everything under the sun they'd have to squeeze into just one. They'd not have one minute to waste, never mind the several Matthew had spent walking Bea back to Dorrie's front door.

At the narrow passage that divided their house from the neighbouring one, Matthew hesitated, watching Tessa thoughtfully through a curtain of snow that was falling even more densely now.

'What's the matter, Tess? I thought you'd be pleased to see me.'

'I am.' She looked at him. 'But one week, Matthew. It's not enough.'

'It has to be. It's all I've got.' He reached an arm around her shoulders.

'Come on. Has Ma still got ears like donkeys' or might I get a cup of tea in peace?'

'Not a chance.' Tessa half turned to smile at him over her shoulder as she led the way round to the back door. 'You know she'll want every detail.'

'Down to what I had for breakfast this

morning, I shouldn't wonder,' Matthew groaned. 'Let's just hope our Hillie's got that kettle on.'

Predictably they'd barely crossed the threshold when Esme surfaced from her doze, sitting bolt upright to start firing a barrage of questions at her son.

'Let him at least get his coat off first,' Tessa admonished, for all their sakes forcing herself to keep her tone mild, but Esme took no such care as she turned to glance scathingly at her daughter-in-law.

'When you've a son you've not seen hide nor hair of in months, happen your opinion might be worth listening to, silly girl.'

'Ma, don't start,' Matthew sighed.

'Me, I'm starting nowt,' Esme stated. 'I'm a ma wanting to know her son's been fed and looked after, that's all.' Briefly her frosty glance ran the length of Tessa. 'There's some of us been sitting here thinking o' nowt else, while others of us been gadding about town in our finery as if we've no husband to fret about ... '

She'd not take the bait, Tessa told herself firmly. No matter what trouble Esme tried to stir up, she'd be trying a long time before she succeeded in pushing Matthew and Tessa apart. If anything her caustic comments had the exact opposite effect.

But when she glanced across at him, the look in Matthew's eyes was briefly accusing before he turned away.

'Tea,' Hilary announced flatly, depositing the cosy-covered pot onto the table. 'I'll leave you to pour, Tess. I'm off to bed.'

'Early yet, Hillie,' Esme cut in. 'You've not seen your brother in months. One cup of tea with him you can manage.'

In the flickering light from the fire, Tessa saw the expression on Hilary's face, such the opposite of what she'd seen when she'd left her with Victoria earlier.

It'd be worry over Leo, she thought. With the sky swelling with the threat of yet more snow, she'd be terrified he'd not make it back for Christmas.

'I'll see to the tea,' she told her quietly, and Hilary smiled her thanks, but it was a smile that didn't quite reach her eyes.

'Leo will walk here if he has to,' Matthew added, and Hilary threw him a brief nod before turning from all of them to trudge slowly up the stairs.

'Not him she's in a stew about,' Esme stated. 'It's the little one.'

'Victoria? She's here safe and sound,' Matthew pointed out.

'Safe and sound and full o' beans about the marvellous Granny Peg,' Esme corrected him. 'Knocked our Hillie well and truly off her pedestal, she has.'

'Poor Hillie,' Matthew murmured. 'Still, it must ease her mind knowing Victoria's happy and cared for.'

'What I told her,' Esme agreed triumphantly. 'Day our Vic comes back with tales of kipping in a cowshed is the day she'll have something to bleat about.'

'She's her mother, Esme.' Tessa regarded the old lady coldly. 'She's had to go without seeing her for four whole months when they'd not been apart since the day Victoria was born. Hillie's every right to be upset if she feels like she's being replaced.'

'Back on your high horse, my girl?' Esme challenged. 'And something else you know nowt about, since your own ma were that fond of you she left you when you were no more than a babby!'

★   ★   ★

At this hour there was no harm in sitting out on the back doorstep, dipping the toes of her shoes to make patterns in the freshly fallen snow.

With everyone else in bed, the fire was out and the gas lamp switched off; not even the smallest chink of light to alert a passing warden.

In the darkness her hearing was as sharp as a rabbit's. Matthew barely made a sound as he descended the stairs and crossed the back room, but Tessa knew his footsteps. She'd know them any-where.

He sat down beside her, tucking the

blanket he carried around her.

'I miss the very bones of you, Tessa Lane,' he told her gently, and she rested her head on his shoulder.

The Truth About Lil

Victoria's cheeks were flushed with the cold but sheer exhilaration shone in her eyes as she patted handfuls of snow into place to mould the shape of the snowman Matthew was helping her to build.

Setting the tea cosy she'd knitted as a Christmas present for Esme back over the pot, Tessa paused for a moment to watch the merriment taking place outside in the garden.

To hear Victoria's shouts oflaughter as she pelted Matthew with snowballs, it was hard to believe that by this time tomorrow she'd be on her way back to Wales, and Granny Peg.

For much of the past week it had been undecided whether she'd be going back at all. Lulled into a false sense of security by the absence of the bombings they'd been told to expect, or any other real signs of war, Hilary had decided there was no danger in keeping Victoria here, where she belonged.

Much of the country was thinking along the same lines, if newspaper stories and reports on the wireless could be believed, London in particular bad seen the return of a good many evacuees.

'To keep her safe I'd not think twice,' Hilary stated quietly. 'But I'll not be parted from my daughter when there's no need for it.'

Even on such an emotive subject it wasn't her way to shout and stamp her feet, but in her voice Tessa for one could hear the growing tenacity that had taken root the moment she'd been coerced into saying goodbye to Victoria four months earlier.

At the time Hilary had seen the sense in it, but aside from the visual preparations of sandbagged buildings and blacked out windows, life had carried on as usual, and she was at a loss as to why it had been for the best that she'd sent her daughter straight into the arms of Granny Peg.

For once, Leo stood firm against his wife. From Lancashire he'd made it home in spite of the snow, but in the New Year he was bound for France.

'You know what I'm heading into, Hillie. This war's anything but over. You'd be best off sending Victoria back where we know she's safe. Least for the time being.'

'We'll all be better off,' Esme piped up. 'Eats like a growing lad, our Vic does. Once this rationing lark kicks in we'll be left with nowt but crumbs if we've to feed her out of it.'

Victoria herself clinched it when she presented Hilary with a picture she'd drawn of the kittens recently born to Granny Peg's cat, Mrs Whiskers.

'See that one,' she said, pointing out the one she'd drawn tumbling head over tail, 'that's mine, Granny Peg said I could name her so I called her Scrapes 'cause she's always getting in them, and see that one,' pointing to a smaller one she'd drawn with big, soulful eyes, 'she's got eyes like yours only green, not hazel, but I called her

Hazel anyway, after you, and Granny Peg says I've to cuddle Hazel when I'm missing you, and I'm to tell you she'll make up her granddaughter's old room so-you can come and see the kittens ... '

'Smelly little scraps, kittens are,' Esme stated, and Hilary had only to catch a glimpse of the weary expression on Victoria's face for her mind to be made up.

* * *

Waving her off for a second time would be hard nonetheless and now she was down to her last few hours with her daughter, Hilary was on her hands and. knees scrubbing out the stove while Victoria charged around the garden with Uncle Matthew.

He'd be leaving tomorrow, too, as would Leo. By the time the sun set on the second day of the New Year, their house would once more be missing half its occupants.

'Are you taking that tea out to them?'

Esme's voice broke into Tessa's thoughts. 'Stone cold it'll be if you stand there brooding on it much longer. Just mind you don't have that door wide open — bitter it is out there and ifit gets in here it'll sit on my chest.'

Closing the door on the torrent of coughing that she knew to be at least partly forced, Tessa picked her way gently amongst mounds of snow that she and Matthew had long since shovelled aside to create a roughly hewn path from the house to the shelter at the very bottom of the garden.

'Ah, tea,' he announced, jamming the-Shovel upright into the snow.

'Sorry, Sprout, your uncle Matthew needs to thaw for five minutes. Ta, Tess.'

'You too, Victoria,' Tessa told her. 'Warm you up a bit, it will. You'll be turning into a snowman yourself, else.'

Victoria took the cup Tessa handed to her, wrapping her wet mittens aronnd it. 'Ta. We've nearly done, Tess. Look. Uncle Matthew says all it needs are Granny's teeth ...'

'Uncle Matthew is old enough to be behaving himself,' Tessa replied sternly, but when he grinned at her she felt her face relax into a smile. 'You'll have her in bother with Esme if you're not careful.'

'She's got too wise a head on her to go blabbing to Granny, haven't you, Sprout?'

It was telling, Tessa thought, that while Victoria took offence at being labelled *our Vic* by Esme, she'd no qualms about the no more flattering nickname Matthew had called her since she was a babby.

Draining her tea, Victoria handed her empty cup back to Tessa. 'Is Ma coming out to see, Tess?'

'She's scrubbing the stove at the minute, bab.' Tessa picked her words cautiously, her eyes meeting Matthew's as the knowledge of why Hillie was ranking the state of the stove above spending precious hours with her daughter passed silently between them. 'She'll perhaps come out when she's done.'

Subdued now, Victoria regarded her solemnly. 'Granny will have her doing something else by then. What about Pa?'

'How about you help me finish off this chap?' Matthew cut in, attempting to save Tessa from having to explain that, with less than a day before he was due to be shipped out to fight in France, Leo had disappeared to the Black Horse rather than face his wife's fear as well as his own, but as ever the astute Victoria refused to be distracted.

'He's not back yet then, and Ma's too busy.'

Tessa stooped a little so she was eye to eye with her niece.

'They have different ways of being brave, that's all. If your ma cleans the kitchen, she's too busy to think about how much she'll miss you, and your pa's gone out for a bit because being here reminds him how much he'll miss the pair of you.'

'Nicely put,' Matthew murmured in her ear. 'You'd make a cracking mother, Tess.'

'So to be brave you've to keep away from people you'll miss and not think about them,' Victoria surmised flatly. 'But you and Uncle Matthew don't do that.'

'Bit different for us, Sprout,' Matthew began, and Victoria nodded wisely.

'I know. 'Cause of how much you love Tess.'

'Not quite what I meant,' he said quietly, glancing at Tessa. 'But true all the same.'

* * *

Departing Birmingham for a second time, Victoria was accompanied by her pa, Uncle Matthew and Aunty Bea, the two of them bound for Norfolk having promised Hilary they'd divert to Wales first to escort her daughter to Granny Peg's doorstep.

Spared the job of delivering her niece on to the train this time round, Tessa had no need to call on the goodwill of Dorrie Cooper and was at the factory in good time to clock on with Lil and the rest.

She'd had every intention of going to

New Street anyway to wave off the four of them, but Matthew had talked her out of it.

'Best you're not there, Tess,' he said, a slight tremble in his voice.

'Hard enough getting on that train knowing I've to watch Brum get smaller behind me twice as hard if I've left you on the platform.'

She'd had to settle for an early morning farewell before she'd left for work, her heart heavy with the knowledge that when she returned that evening, Matthew would be gone.

Lil she looked to as a timely distraction. She'd seen her just once over the Christmas week, when Matthew and Bertie had caught up for a drink at the Black Horse, and she'd noted the way Lil's face had been glowing brighter than a candle flame. She'd be full of her Christmas with Bertie and bursting to tell every minute of it.

Sure enough, a morning of running up the first batch of a new order for Women's Air Force uniforms to the accompaniment of Lil's endless chatter and by the time they broke for lunch Tessa already knew the ins and outs of her friend's Christmas, down to how many chestnuts Dorrie had used to make the stuffing.

But she was to find that Lil had saved the most important detail til last.

'Enough of me and my tales though,' she ventured, when they were sitting in the canteen, eating their lunch. 'What about you, Mrs Lane? Not surprised you kept Matthew under your hat for so long. He's lovely.'

Her heart twisting at the thought that he'd be well on his way back to barracks by now, Tessa forced a thin smile.

'He's my closest friend, Lil. Nothing more.'

'Just your husband,' Lil countered. 'He clearly thinks the world of you in any case.' She paused, scraping up the last of her mashed potato on to her fork.

'Bea's a treasure, isn't she? She were telling me how she's had to put her hand to all sorts, from being in charge of them barrage balloons to learning how to read

131

radar signals.'

'A world away from sitting at a sewing machine day after day,' Tessa sighed, and Lil eyed her curiously.

'So says Brum's most devoted dressmaker. You do your bit, Tess. We all do. Them uniforms don't sew themselves now, do they? I'll say one thing for those WAAF tunics — they're a deal easier to grapple with than that rough serge they make the chaps wear.'

Tessa pushed her half eaten meal away. 'Bea and I, we always said we'd join up together.'

'Keep an eye on her then, couldn't you?' Lil commented easily. 'Make sure she's not after turning Matthew's head.'

'She's not. Nor is he after having it turned.'

Lil smiled at the stiffness of Tessa's tone. 'I know that, Tess. There for all the world to see, it was.' She paused, absent-mindedly crumbling the currants out of her cake. 'You've no business upping and leaving me now, anyway, Tessa Lane. Not when I've a favour so important I'd trust none but you to do it.'

Tessa glanced up at her, a sudden suspicion forming when she saw the excitement that made Lil's eyes sparkle.

'You want me to dispose of Bertie's piano so he has eyes for you only,' she teased her, and the smile on Lil's face widened.

'No, Tess. I want you to make my wedding dress.'

She should have seen that one coming, Tessa thought later as she wandered home, her spirits lightened a little at the prospect of making something so important for her friend, but not quite enough to completely soothe the ache she felt knowing she was moments away from walking. into a house that no longer contained Matthew.

The thought of Lil and Bertie's wedding, as much of a welcome distraction as the preparations would no doubt prove to be, was as yet tinged with a bittersweet edge.

It was only to be expected she'd compare their fate to hers, she reasoned to herself. She and Matthew may not love each other in the same way as did Lil and Bertie, but she loved him all the same and they'd been forced apart while Lil and Bertie would start their married life very much together.

She could just imagine what Esme would make of it, the clipped comparisons she'd be sure to voice. Tessa groaned inwardly as she walked quietly along the passageway and rolled to the back door. As with every other day, the longer the old lady was pennitted to sleep undisturbed, the easier it was for everyone.

On opening the back door, however, she found the house to be in darkness.

No light flickered from the gas lamp and the absence of a fire in the grate left a chill so raw it made Tessa shiver.

Where was Hilary? Surely she'd not gone to bed at this early hour?

What of Esme? In the brief moment Tessa stood still as a statue, her mind racing with all manner of dreadful possibilities, there was no sound from the armchair in the corner.

But when she forced herself to move silently towards the mantel and with trembling fingers lit the candlewick, a familiar voice startled her into almost dropping the match.

'Took your time, my girl! Off gallivanting, no doubt, and me sat here with the cold in my chest so much I'll be lucky if I live to see another Christmas ...'

Warily, Tessa regarded Esme in the flickering light from the candle.

'Where's Hilary got to?'

Suddenly she felt sure Esme would tell her that Hilary had left them too, that she'd caught the train with Victoria, when it came down to it unable to be parted a second time from her daughter.

Esme sniffed her annoyance. 'Off down the town hall, she is. Some women's volunteer group. Excuse for a cackle of busybodies to lark about and drink tea, I call it.'

For Hilary's sake Tessa attempted to conceal her surprise rather than unwittingly fuel Esme's resentment.

'Women's Voluntary Service,' she supplied. 'They've mobile canteens dotted around Brum pots of tea on the go for servicemen and the like.'

'If she's after making pots of tea she's no need to go further than this here kitchen!' Esme spluttered. 'Unless she'd rather brew up for a bunch of strangers than her own ma!'

'I'll just stoke the fire up a bit then I'll make you a cup,' Tessa sighed, but she'd barely knelt down by the hearth before Esme's sharp rebuke stopped her in her tracks.

'Fat lot of good it is now I'm already frozen through to me bones.'

'All the more reason you should have a fire to warm you up a bit,' Tessa replied patiently, but Esme was having none of it.

'No sense in it we'll be in our beds directly. Coal don't come cheap, my girl, but then you'll give no thought to that, will you, as it doesn't come out of your pocket.'

Wearily, Tessa rose to her feet. 'I'll get the pot on then.'

Her eyes used to the darkness now, she lit the gas under the kettle and reached for the tea caddy, glad of the chance for two minutes to herself as her mind ticked over.

Was Hilary really down at the town hall brewing urns of tea and sifting through second-hand blankets or had she just told Esme that to cover up the truth, that she'd not be back this evening, or any time soon, because with Granny Peg's offer of making up her granddaughter's old room for her in mind, she was off to catch a train to Wales?

Such reckless spontaneity was as far removed from normal Hilary behaviour as night from day, but so too was leaving her ma alone in the house, especially as she'd not even thought to stoke up the fire for her first.

As a spasm of hacking coughs convulsed Esme's chest, Tessa found herself feeling sorry for the old lady. Bitter, twisted and downright hurtful she might be, but she'd been sitting in a room that was no better than an icebox for a good few hours if the long since smouldered ashes in that grate were anything to go by.

The pot boiled, Tessa was mashing the tea leaves when she heard Hilary's light step along the passageway outside.

'She's back then, is she?' Esme remarked, as Hilary stood in the kitchen, stamping her feet and blowing on her hands, for the moment paying no heed at all to her ma.

'Arctic out there,' she declared briskly, as if she'd merely popped out to use the privy. 'Glad you've got a pot made, Tess.'

She'd a strange look in her eyes, Tessa noted. A kind of wild excitement, the joy of tasting freedom and coming back drunk on it. Not unlike the look she'd seen in Lil's eyes when she'd first set foot on Birmingham soil.

'You've been helping out at the town hall then,' she ventured, and Hilary nodded, unwinding the soft woollen scarf Tessa had knitted from around her neck.

'They've a clothing exchange up and running. Coats and blankets and all sorts.

138

Me and another woman had the job of sorting through today's donations.'

It'd be helping to take her mind off how quiet the house was without Victoria, or what was lying in wait for Leo across the Channel, Tessa thought.

Not that Hilary had ever been at liberty to think much beyond Esme's constant stream of demands. Running round after her ma, her days had been all consuming. The difference now was the blame she'd placed squarely at Esme's door.

Tessa knew it, as did Matthew. A week of watching Hilary struggle over what was best for Victoria, and they'd seen the silent contempt she'd aimed at her ma for putting her in this position to begin with.

Not down to Esme Lane that there was a war on and children having to be evacuated to safety, of course, but down to her that Victoria had left having long since accepted that in this house Granny pulled all the strings; that Hilary wasn't free to put her daughter first and foremost, and that Victoria herself had learnt to watch every word in case it set Granny off with a bee in her bonnet.

The relative peace and freedom of Granny Peg's house, with its brood of kittens, and a substitute grandmother who considered Victoria's feelings, she couldn't be blamed for favouring.

Watching Hilary calmly stir milk into her tea while a few feet away Esme spluttered into another fit of coughing, Tessa knew her sister-in-law's days of jumping to attention were a thing of the past. Esme was no longer a distraction but a constant reminder of why Victoria had willingly returned to stay with Granny Peg.

Her own guilt that she'd let Esme dictate for so long no less tangible, it was little wonder that with the stove scrubbed to within an inch of its life, Hilary was finally looking elsewhere to divert her thoughts and fill the emptiness she felt without Leo and Victoria by her side.

She'd not turn away from her ma completely, though. In seconds of clocking the shivering figure in the faint light given off by the candle, in a room starkly devoid of the glow of firelight, she'd fetched a blanket which she tucked securely around Esme's thin shoulders.

★   ★   ★

In the weeks that followed, Tessa was grateful to have her own escape in the shape of Lil and her wedding preparations. Throughout a bitterly cold January as steeped in snow as December had been, their Saturday afternoon jaunt to the Bull Ring was quickly abandoned in favour of tea, cakes and endless chat by the fire in Ginny Cirelli's sitting room.

Once the snow finally started to melt, they braved the cold once more to stock up on the materials Tessa needed to make Lil's dress, but from then on, aside from the odd trip into town for a browse and a custard slice, Saturday afternoons were given to planning and stitching.

Truth be told Tessa could have made up Lil's frock in a fraction of the time, as she'd confessed to her more than once, but with the miserable weather and the dreaded rationing conspiring to put the mockers on her big day, until the sun put in an appearance at least Lil was in no particular hurry, and for her part, Tessa was only too happy to lose herself in a pastime she enjoyed so much.

'Must bring back memories, all this,' Lil ventured one afternoon, glancing up from her scrutiny of Tessa's collection of white and pearl buttons to catch her friend's eye. 'Less than a year and you've another posh white frock to fuss over.'

Laid gently across Tessa's lap was Lil's dress, into the hem of which she was stitching delicate cream lace flowers. Stilling her needle a moment, she looked across at the future Mrs Cooper.

'Not quite the same, Lil. Two evenings at the most it took me to have that old frock looking presentable, and when it was done I gave it no more thought.'

'Bertie says you looked a treat in it,' Lil said, her eyes sparkling, and Tessa shook her head in disbelief.

'Bertie says far too much, in my view.'

'He says he'll have none other than Matthew as his best man,' Lil continued, raising her eyebrows pointedly at Tessa. 'So you'd best get writing to that husband of yours.'

'I do,' Tessa replied, her tone mildly indignant. 'Every week.'

Lil nodded, as if she'd expected nothing less. 'You'll have told him about your Hilary, then?'

She had, yes. Coming home to that house with no Matthew there had been hard enough; coming home each night to find no Hilary, either, until a much later hour in any case, and Esme striking up a chorus of coughing and complaining, no matter if the fire was sweltering and the tea freshly poured, Tessa had long since confided the whole sorry tale.

Not that she'd willingly give him more to fret about. She'd never write another word rather than upset him, but writing to Matthew and leaving out the bits that troubled her felt stilted and unnatural. Indeed she'd worried him more the one time she'd tried it anyway, and he'd written back imploring her to talk to him as she'd always been able to.

'I tell Matthew everything,' she said softly. 'Always have.'

'Just friends or not, you couldn't be closer,' Lil agreed. 'Then there's me and Bertie, head over heels sweet on each other, and I've yet to tell him half of it.'

She kept her tone light but the pre-occupied expression on her face as she studiously avoided Tessa's eyes by fixing her attention on a sightless rummage through the button tin told a different story.

Laying her sewing aside, Tessa recalled Bertie's suspicions about Lil's mother, as she'd done so many times over the past weeks, wondering about her friend whose past, whoever it concerned, she'd yet to confide.

She recalled too her own initial suspicions of months ago when Lil had been little more than a mysterious stranger. The blase way she'd waltzed off the train and into an unfamiliar city when she'd been none the wiser where she'd be laying her head that first night, and on the eve of war!

'Lil, I've known Bertie since he were a little lad,' Tessa began. 'Whatever you've to tell him, it'll make no odds. There's nothing you can say that'll have him running for the hills ...'

'Me who did the running, Tess,' Lil sighed. 'Meant to be a new start, it was. Off to the bright lights of Brum to seek my fortune.'

'You'll be lucky.' Tessa smiled at her, but the smile Lil managed in return fell miles short of her usual exuberant beam.

'Five minutes I'd been here and Bertie were on at me to sing with him.'

'He'd not have meant any offence,' Tessa said softly. 'It's just Bertie's way. He sees an inn full of folk and he's duty bound to whip 'em up into a rousing chorus.'

'Has help to do it now, doesn't he?' Lil reminded her. 'Tess, I told you I couldn't sing a note and then come Christmas I was at Bertie's side singing my heart out.' Her forehead wrinkled in consternation.

'I lied to you.'

'You'll have had your reasons.'

Lil nodded 'You heard of Marianne Foster, Tess? No? Professional singer, West End star ... and my aunt.'

In the event that Bertie's theory had been spot on, Tessa had thought it best to assume ignorance, to let Lil confide however much she wished in her own time, but with the revelation that Marianne was not her mother but her aunt, she struggled for a moment to conceal her surprise.

'Runs in the family then,' she managed eventually. 'This singing talent of yours.'

Lil smiled wistfully. 'When I was little, Gran would have us all gathered round the piano — me; my ma and Aunty Mai. She'd play and the three of us would sing together.'

'Does your ma sing professionally, too?'

'That was the plan,' Lil sighed. 'She and Aunty Mai were twins, Tess. Identical down to the last freckle and both able to sing like angels.'

'Were?' Tessa echoed, an unsettled feeling in the pit of her stomach as she waited for Lil to continue.

'Ma copped it when I was little,' Lil said briskly. 'Tuberculosis. A matter of weeks and she was dead and buried.'

Tessa caught her breath so sharply it made her chest ache. 'I'm sorry, Lil.'

'Aunty Mai went off anyway,' Lil continued as if she'd not heard. 'Her name up in lights and all of London's high society hearing her sing.' She shook her head slowly. 'Pretty life she made for herself, while it lasted.'

'What happened?' Tessa enquired, expecting to hear something along the lines of Marianne Foster's fame, however great, having been fleeting as London's high society turned their attention to a newer model.

'Ate herself into an early grave,' Lil replied bluntly. 'Or rather she didn't. Got it in her head she'd have to be thin as a rake if she were to keep dazzling folk. She'd been eating next to nothing for months first time she visited Gran and me. It were too late to save her.'

Tessa exhaled heavily. 'Oh, Lil.'

'Three of us down to one,' Lil continued. 'I'm all that's left, see. Down to me to light up the stage and put a smile back on Gran's face.'

Reeling as she was, suddenly Tessa understood. 'But you've no interest in singing professionally.'

Lil shook her head. 'Gran's dream, Tess. Not mine. I'm not my ma, nor am I Aunty Mai. Why I came here, so I could just be me.'

'You obviously love singing, though,' Tessa ventured tentatively, recalling the joy in Lil's eyes that first night she'd took her place at Bertie's side.

The first of the tears spilled out as Lil smiled sadly. 'I loved my mother, Tess. Aunty Mai, too.'

It wasn't just a case of stretching her own wings, Tessa realised as she crossed to Lil's side to hold her close for a minute, but more that she'd been locking out anything that reminded her of her ma and her aunty.

Only when she'd heard from Tessa that Bertie would love her if she was never to sing a note had she felt able to do so, relieved of the pressure her gran had put upon her to carry on the legacy of the Foster sisters.

'You should tell Bertie,' Tessa advised her gently. 'He'd want you to turn to him, Lil.'

She nodded, smiling bravely through her tears. 'He's already asked if I've family to speak of, you know, for the wedding invitations.'

'Will you be inviting your gran?' Tessa asked cautiously. 'I know you've reason not to ...'

'But she's got no say over my life,' Lil finished. 'I know, Tess. She'd no say over it last year when I left to move here either.'

Her gaze dropped to the button tin, and absentmindedly she raked up handfuls, letting them fall slowly back through her fingers with a clatter. 'My gran's the kindest woman you'd ever hope to meet,

Tess. She'll not push me into anything. She never did.'

'But ... ' Tessa stared at her, bewildered. 'Then why'd you leave her?'

Lil shook her head incredulously, as though the answer to that was as plain as day. 'I'm the spit of them, Tess. She looks at me, she sees her dreams shattered. For both our sakes I had to leave. I can't spend the rest of my life being a disappointment.'

Chances are she'd cease to be any such thing the minute her gran heard her sing with Bertie, Tessa mused as she wandered home later. Friday night singsongs in the Black Horse might be a World away from the glitz and glamour of the West End stage, but the folk hereabouts who crowded the inn to bursting point couldn't have loved her more if she'd been dolled up in sequins and hobnobbing with London's elite.

But Lil would not be swayed into writing to her gran. Once she'd confided the whole story to Tessa, aside from the necessary relaying of it to Bertie she'd no more to say on the subject, quietly but firmly resisting any attempts either of them made to talk it over with her.

Understanding only too well the pain of raking over such a loss as Lil had suffered, Tessa allowed it to be swept under the carpet and their Saturday afternoon conversations reverted to dress measurements and the challenge of making a wedding cake with both butter and sugar on the ration.

Stepping up as the fairy godmother of the hour was Ginny Cirelli, whose cooking prowess Lil had long since been praising.

'Give that woman crumbs and she'll turn them into a banquet,' she declared, happy to delegate the responsibility for the centrepiece of her wedding breakfast onto her landlady's shoulders.

As enchanted by Lillian Foster as was the rest of Birmingham, Ginny was more than happy to do it. Indeed she'd her own reasons for being glad of the distraction, as Lil confided to Tessa.

'She's fretting over her Alec, in case

he gets carted off.' She sniffed crossly. 'Chap like him, never done anyone a moment's harm, they've no business hounding him. You know what his name means, Tess? Alessandro — protector of mankind, and hasn't he done just that, taking the likes of me in under his roof, but just because he's Italian he's having to look over his shoulder every minute of the day ... '

If she'd come to Birmingham searching for a replacement family, Lil had found it and more besides, Tessa thought. The Cirellis in particular she looked to as substitute parents, though with the tide of favour indeed turning against Italians, Bertie confided he'd be happier once his Lil had her feet safely under Dorrie's table.

With the wedding finally booked for the second week of June, Tessa was able to write to Matthew with a definite date, heading back home once she'd posted the letter to find the wireless on and Hilary there for a change, both she and Esme sitting in stunned silence.

'It's started proper, Tess,' Hilary said quietly. 'They're saying the phoney war's over and now it's all for real.'

'We're all for it, mark my words,' Esme declared. 'Whole country will have copped it by Christmas. Maybe I was wrong to make you send our Vic away, Hillie. Looks like she'll be as safe here as anywhere.'

Hilary's eyes flashed fire as she fixed them on her mother. 'You didn't make me do anything, Ma, and since we're on the subject, my daughter's name is Victoria.'

Made a change, Tessa thought, Esme being lost for words. Be the shock, she reasoned, with the perpetrator being the one she'd have least expected to stand up to her.

'I'll get the pot on to boil then, shall I?' As if she'd not stunned her mother into silence, Hilary got to her feet and strode purposefully into the kitchen.

Left with just Tessa, Esme scrabbled to regain the upper hand by diverting her scathing glance on to her daughter-in-law.

'My Mattie will be lucky if he sees the end of this rotten war ... '

In that moment Tessa hated her. 'He's not *your Mattie*,' she said coldly.

'He's my Matthew, and he'll be coming home safe and in one piece.'

★   ★   ★

She was at Dorrie's flat a few days later, having a cup of tea with Bertie, while Lil helped her future mother-in-law try on the blouse Tessa had embroidered with tiny cream flowers to match Lil's frock for the big day.

Waiting for a concert by a dance band he liked, Bertie switched on the wireless in good time to catch the news broadcast that preceded it, and Tessa heard the words that made her go cold with terror.

Norfolk had seen its first bombing of the war ... on the Royal Air Force base at West Raynham.

'But You Don't Love Me, Tess …'

Dawn had barely broken as Tessa hurried along Hockley Street, her steps echoing in the stillness of first light. They'd hours yet before they were due to arrive at the church, but she knew Lil would have been up a fair while already.

She'd been so excited the night before she'd vowed she'd not be able to sleep at all, but Tessa knew pure vanity if nothing else would have had her catching a few hours. Not for Lil a glide down the aisle with shadows under her eyes!

This early it was so quiet, as if the world had yet to wake up. Such peace was deceptive, Tessa.thought sadly. Here in this very moment, under a pink streaked sunrise, welcomed by the morning calls of a chorus of birds, and the curl of factory smoke as Birmingham went about its business as usual, you'd not think there was a war on.

It was creeping closer though. She'd only to walk through the door of the Cirellis' and even though they'd be putting a brave face on it for Lil's sake, the strain they'd been under since Italy had come in on the side of the Germans was etched in both their faces.

Ginny was terrified her husband would be arrested and though he did his best to reassure her, the fear in Alec Cirelli's eyes showed plainly he was waiting for the doorbell to ring.

They'd had no trouble as yet, but Lil's presence under their roof was an endless source of worry for Bertie all the same. He'd wanted her to move into Bea's room and he'd stop with the Cirellis' until the wedding, but Lil was having none of it.

After today she'd be living in Dorrie's flat but until then she'd not turn her back on Ginny.

As much as she liked the Cirellis, Tessa understood Bertie's desperate need to know that Lil was safe. All too close a memory were the days and nights she'd spent beside herself with fear, sleep impossible and not able to swallow so much as a cup of tea, until Matthew had written to tell her he was safe.

West Raynham had copped a pasting good and proper, and lives had been lost, but Matthew's wasn't one of them. In the ensuing chaos he'd written as soon as he'd been able, and the news that he was all right had left Tessa weak with relief.

It had been too close for comfort, though. This war had rubbed shoulders with her Matthew, and in the weeks since, she'd been so constantly on edge that every day had left her exhausted by the end of it.

She'd be seeing him in a few hours. They'd allowed him a forty-eight hour pass so he could come back and be Bertie's best man.

He'd be catching a train from Norfolk this morning and he'd have the best part of tomorrow before he'd have to catch a train back so he'd be there to report for duty the following morning.

Tessa smiled to herself, thinking of the day they had planned tomorrow. *We'll get the tram out to the Lickeys*, Matthew had written, *Just you and me, like old times ...*

Knowing what Tessa had gone through over the past weeks, Dorrie had swung it so she could take the day off from the factory, but she'd have taken it anyway and if she'd lost her job over it she'd not have cared one bit. Jobs were ten a penny with so many going off to fight.

She could always get another job but she'd not get another Matthew.

A spring in her step she'd not felt in a while, Tessa arrived at the Cirellis' front door and knocked softly.

Ever mindful of their constant worry, she'd no intention of rapping on it like an impatient copper. With Lil up and hovering by the window, waiting for her to arrive, the most timid of taps would suffice.

As she'd expected, the door was opened immediately but the Lil who greeted her was so pale-faced she'd no need to utter a word for Tessa to know that all was not well.

Raising a discreet finger to her lips, Lil

beckoned Tessa inside, slipping her arm firmly through hers once she'd closed the door quietly.

'What time do you call this then?' she declared with false brightness. 'Some of us have been up for hours, I'll have you know. We'd best be getting me into my frock if we're to make it to the church on time!'

Only when she'd ushered Tessa into her room and closed the door after them did Lil fill her in and even then she kept her voice low.

'Police are here, Tess. They've got Alec holed up in the sitting room and answering to all sorts.' Anger blazed in her eyes as she shook her head in disbelief. 'Ginny's knocked for six. She'd still got her hair in rags and there they were, on the doorstep at the crack of dawn.'

'Bit early for house calls,' Tessa stated grimly. 'Trying to catch him in, I suppose. So Ginny's got no chance of warning him to scarper.'

Lil shrugged, 'Do them no good. Alec Cirelli's as patriotic as they come. They'll find nothing on him.'

'I know. Pity they've had to barge in on your wedding day to prove it.'

'It'll all blow over in no time,' Lil declared confidently. 'Come eleven o'clock I'll be walking down that aisle with Alec there to give me away, you'll see.'

She wasn't as confident of that as she sounded, Tessa realised, when she caught a glimpse of the shadow that flitted briefly across her face, but it would do none of them any good to dwell on what might be occurring in the Cirellis' sitting room.

They'd be as well to just get on with things, to have Lil dressed and made-up so that when the policemen left them to it, they'd be able to get on with her day as planned.

'Let's get you in that frock then,' Tessa said brightly. 'Be time to go and you'll be traipsing up the aisle in your house-coat, else.'

'Thanks, Tess.' Lil threw her a grateful smile, but as she turned to retrieve her dress from its hanger, the sound of voices in the hall stopped her in her tracks.

Tessa felt she dared not even breathe as she and Lil stood stock still and as quiet as mice, straining to listen to what was being said.

Voices were low and muffled by the solid wood of Lil's bedroom door, but the heated, fractious tone was unmistakeable.

Anger blazed once more in Lil' s eyes, but she remained frozen to the spot.

Only when they heard the front door open did she suddenly dart forward.

'I'm not having this!'

'Lil, no!' Grabbing her arm, Tessa held it fast. 'You go out there shouting the odds, you'll get yourself carted off as well!'

Tears brimmed in Lil's eyes as she stared helplessly at her. 'He's done nothing wrong, Tess.'

'So they've nothing on him, have they?' Tessa reasoned, trying to keep her voice calm when inside she felt anything but. 'Let's just wait and see what Ginny has to say ... '

Barely had the words left her mouth than there was a light tap on the door and when Lil opened it, Ginny Cirelli's ashen face told them all they needed to know.

'Alec told me not to fret,' she murmured shakily. 'Said. I'm to go to your wedding, walk you down the aisle in his place ... ' She caught her breath sharply, stifling a sob. 'I can't do it, Lil, I can't just carry on as if my husband's not been locked up.'

'It's all right, Ginny,' Lil assured her. 'Really it is. You've no need to think of me today. Alec's more important, I understand that.'

As if fortified by Lil's kindness, Ginny straightened up, stiffening her shoulders and taking a deep breath to steady herself.

'He'd tell me I were fretting over nowt, wouldn't he? You know my Alec, he'd not harm a hair on anyone's head, and once them coppers have worked that out for themselves, he'll be back home where he belongs.'

She touched Lil's arm. 'I'd best get myself down that police station. Won't take 'em long to see they've got the wrong man — he'll be out in good time to walk you down that aisle, you see if he's not!'

She knew there was no chance of that happening, Tessa thought, same as Lil did, but where would any of them be if they just shrugged their shoulders and let this blessed war do its worst?

Once the authorities were convinced Alec Cirelli was clean as a whistle he'd be a free man, but while he was under suspicion Tessa couldn't imagine they'd be all that willing to get a move on clearing his name.

End of the day for his release was pushing it — Lil's wedding he'd miss for certain. Ginny needed to hope all the same — she'd not much else she could do.

As for Lil, her attachment to the Cirellis ran deep, but deeper still was her love for Bertie. This was their day, and a pair of interfering coppers had threatened a part of it before the sun was up.

She was determined nonetheless to see out the rest of it with no hitches, but though she put a brave face on it, even managing a smile as she stood in front of the mirror all dolled up in her dress, Tessa knew she was distracted.

'They'd not want your day spoilt over this,' she told her, when, having waited in vain for Ginny at least to return, they arrived at the gates to the churchyard.

'I know that,' Lil replied. 'I'll not let it be spoilt, I promise. I just wish they could be here.' She smiled a suddenly watery smile. 'I wish a lot of people could be here, Tess.'

It was the first time she'd spoken of her family since she'd confided what had happened to her mother, and her Aunty Marianne. Not so final was Alec Cirelli's fate but even so he and Ginny were just two more people she cared for who, albeit through no fault of their own, had left her to go it alone.

Tessa slipped her arm comfortingly

through Lil's. 'You've folk in that church wanting to see you get married. Dorrie, Bea, even Hillie's torn herself away from the clothing exchange for five minutes, and you've got me, who'll walk you down that aisle myself if it'll put a smile on your face!'

Lil smiled obligingly, tucking her arm tightly around Tessa's. 'I'd like that, Tess. Thank you.'

It was a world away from her own wedding day, Tessa couldn't help thinking as she and Lil stepped inside the ornate serenity of the church.

There'd been no graceful glide along the aisle, no months of fussing over every, little detail ... she and Bea had hurried up the steps of the register office, Matthew had put a ring on her finger, and they'd been out again in time for a sandwich and a cuppa before life resumed as normal in the afternoon.

Not that the two days could be compared. Lil and Bertie were in love — it was only right they'd want a bit more fuss than a quick dash to the register office.

Bertie turned to look at Lil as she floated towards him, his face shining with happiness, and to one side of him stood Matthew.

Tessa hadn't seen him since Christmas and in that time he'd come so close to being finished off by a bomb; but here he was, safe and sound. She found she'd a lump in her throat she struggled to swallow as she passed Lil over to Bertie.

Taking a step back from them, she arrived at Matthew's side, and discreetly he reached for her hand and held it tightly.

★ ★ ★

'Bit different to our wedding, Tess,' he said later, as they wandered slowly back to Esme's house.

On leaving the church they'd all gone on to the Black Horse, where Jeannie, the landlady, had whipped up a bit of a spread. As Tessa had feared, there'd been no sign of the Cirellis, but though she faltered a little when she and Bertie cut the cake Ginny had made for them, on the whole Lil had managed to enjoy herself.

Aside from the absence of Alec and Ginny, she'd had the day she wanted.

The elegant dress, the beautiful flowers, the first dance with Bertie to a scing they'd chosen together ...

'No sense in us having all that palaver, was there?' Tessa pointed out, and Matthew sighed softly.

'Suppose not.'

Tessa was just content to have him back by her side as they strolled along in a companionable silence, but after a moment or two Matthew tried again.

'I've done you out of all that palaver as you call it, haven't I? Are you really not fussed?'

'You know me better than that, Matthew,' she returned quietly. 'I've far more important things to worry about, in any case, and if we'd got dolled up to the nines and waltzed around in a fairytale bubble, I'd still have them, wouldn't I?'

'You've a right way of putting things, Tess.' Matthew smiled distractedly, but his voice shook slightly as he took her hand. 'I'm sorry. I wrote as soon as I could. It was just, oh Tess, we took a right pasting. Felt like everything had gone up, just a wall of fire, and men trapped in the rubble ...'

He exhaled slowly. 'I just kept thinking I could have copped it. I'd been in a hangar not two minutes before and it'd got a direct hit — if I'd still been in there I'd have had no chance ... I'd have made you a widow, and for what?'

'But you didn't.' Her own voice trembled as she put her arms around him and held him close. 'You're still here, and I'm telling you now, Matthew Lane, that's the way I want it kept so if you think you're getting back on that train tomorrow you've another think coming.'

If only it were that simple. He'd agree not to go back, and that'd be it, constant fretting all over and done with, and Matthew back home where he belonged, and not on an air base in Norfolk that the enemy pilots knew to target.

If only she could keep him safe without fear of the military police landing on the doorstep and carting him off the same way the coppers had carted off Alec Cirelli.

'What'll you do? Hide me in the coal shed?' Matthew tried a smile, but it didn't quite reach his eyes. 'I've got to go back. You know I have.'

Of course she did. She lmew Matthew had to do his bit to help win the war, same as she did, same as they all did.

Flying planes or stitching the uniforms the pilots flew them in, everyone had to Pitch in. She'd just have to take comfort that, being in Ground Crew, he'd keep two feet firmly on dry land.

'Least you're not risking your neck going up in them planes,' she reasoned, trying hard for his sake to return her voice to normal, but Matthew just sighed sadly, tightening his hold on her as they stood for a minute in the street outside Esme's house.

'I'm not going back yet, Tess. We've

got tomorrow.'

They had the best part of it, in any case, and she was determined they'd not waste a minute. She'd have to stand on that platform while he got on the train, and this time she'd not be talked out of it, so until then for his sake even more than hers she'd smile and make the most of it. He'd be snatched back into the cll.ltches of war soon enough — he deserved a few precious hours of not having to think about it.

★   ★   ★

Up with the lark the following morning, they'd left the house in good time to pick up the first tram bound for the edge of Birmingham, and the Lickey Hills.

'Channing, that is,' Esme had grumbled. 'Not back five minutes and he's flitting off with her ladyship when he's not seen his own ma for months on end.'

Standing up to her ma more and more since she'd started serving tea to the

Home Guard and rifling through folks' cast offs, Hilary had defended them.

'He's every right to want to spend the day with Tess. They're married, remember.'

Esme had snorted derisively. 'Not proper, they ain't. Makes a mockery o' folk like me and my Arthur. Now we had what you call a proper marriage — you've nowt like it with that one, Mattie.'

'Thank heavens for that,' Matthew had muttered under his breath, one arm around Tessa's waist steering her towards the door.

Despite how determined he was to squeeze out every last minute of today, Matthew was distracted, his gaze fixed on the passing familiar sights but seeing none of them as they travelled towards the Lickeys.

Tessa was glad she'd got him out of the house, at least. The way Hilary had stood up for them against her ma was testimony to the quiet strength she seemed to glean from the hours she spent every day helping out with the WVS, but with soldiers being shipped back from the beaches of Dunkirk and Leo yet to appear among them, the part of her holding on to every last shred of hope that he'd made it out alive waited with nerves as taut as telephone wire to hear the rattle of the letter box.

Then there was Esme, tutting and shaking her head over Leo's chances of turning up in one piece, though she at least had the sense to do it when her Hillie was out of earshot.

Tessa didn't want Matthew to be around any of it.

He'd feel better once they'd got there, she reasoned. Passing through Brum, on all sides they were faced with signs of war, but the Lickeys would be as they'd always been, green, fresh and undisturbed, an escape from the day to day drudge.

They'd walk round the lake, and up into the woods where the pungent scent of the pine trees chased away the city smog, where they'd walked a hundred times, and Matthew would feel better.

'I'm sorry, Tess,' he said quietly, as arm in arm they wandered through the trees. 'I'll perk up a bit, I promise.'

'It's all right,' she assured him, but he shook his head firmly.

'No, it isn't. It's not all right, any of it.'

Tessa had no intention of patronising him by claiming different, even to try to soothe his agitated spirits. They both knew how it was; a few hours from now he'd be off and swallowed up once more by this war, and she'd be back to fretting every moment of every day, so no, things were about as far from all right as they'd ever be.

If they spent these precious hours dwelling on it though, all they'd be left with later was the sorrow and regret of knowing; they'd wasted this rare day together.

'You'll not change a thing by fretting on it all day,' she said softly.

'Either way you'll be leaving me soon enough so we've nothing to lose by treasuring each other's company for a few hours, like we used to.'

'Before I dragged you off to the register office, you mean?' There was a trace of bitterness in his tone that made her heart sink.

'Way I remember it, I walked there on my own two feet,' she countered, and he sighed irritably.

'You know what I mean.' He came to a standstill, gazed around him as if seeing it all for the first time. 'Not been back here since the day I proposed, have we? Only fitting we should be here again so I can put it right.'

'Put it right?' Tessa echoed. 'What's wrong about it?'

Matthew's eyes met hers and he spoke flatly. 'I've not been fair to you. I'd no right pushing you into marrying me.'

'I'd not have gone through with it if I'd any doubts,' she replied softly, but he appeared not to hear her, sinking down onto the grass and leaning back against a tree trunk, closing his eyes with a sigh.

'They're sending me up, Tess.'

She felt cold suddenly, chilled to the bone. 'But ... they can't ... you're ground crew ...'

'We lost pilots when we were bombed,' Matthew explained. 'There's a fair few of us being trained up to fly in their place.' Forcing his eyes open, he fixed them on her. 'I've trapped you to me, Tess. Any day I could end up on the wrong end of a bomb, or at the bottom of the Channel ...'

'Don't say things like that.' She frowned at him. 'I'd no need of a ring on my finger to be worried about you night and day, if that's what you're getting at.'

He nodded, accepted the truth in What she was saying. 'I'd be putting you through it anyway, wouldn't I?'

'Nothing we can do about that,' she said softly, and he reached for her hand and held it tightly.

'I know. Same for me, Tess. Point is, I'd not half the reason to fret about you as I made out, had I? Job you do, stitching them uniforms, if that don't count as war work, I don't know what does. You'll not be called up, not in a month of Sundays.'

She'd not thought of it like that. 'Suppose not.'

'I knew you'd not have to go anywhere,' Matthew continued, averting his eyes from hers. 'I'd no business marrying you, Tess.'

Tessa stared at him, her thoughts in turmoil. What was he trying to say? That he regretted marrying her? That he'd some other reason for doing so he'd yet to confess to her?

'So why'd you do it then?' she managed, to her own ears the tremble in her voice as clear as a bell. 'Was it to keep me from joining up with Bea? If I decide to go, you've no say in it, Matthew.'

He turned to look at her. 'I'd not expect to have. All the same, I'd still rather you didn't.'

'Like I didn't want you flitting off to join up before this war had even started,' Tessa retorted bitterly. 'Still went though, didn't you? Never mind that this ring might mean the same to me as it does to you.'

Her voice caught, and she swallowed hard. 'Do you know what I went through when West Raynharn was bombed, not knowing if you were alive or dead? You married me and you got what you wanted out of it — you know I'm here and safe,' she finished flatly. 'I'd give anything to be able to say the same.'

Matthew stared evenly back at her, a silent challenge in his hazel eyes.

'But you don't love me, Tess. Not proper you don't. That's why you're not fussed we never had all the trimmings Lil and Bertie had. They'd a right to every bit of it but you and me ... ' he shook his head increduously. 'Ma's right. It makes a mockery of the whole thing.'

'I've yet to see the day when Esme is right about anything,' Tessa declared heatedly. 'She can get herself in a lather about it all she likes and it'll not take away the nights I've not slept for worrying, nor will it mean there's anyone else in this world who means more to me than you do, Matthew Lane!'

'But you don't love me,' he repeated.

'Only proper reason to get married, Tess. Nothing else comes close.'

Leaning back against the tree trunk with a sigh, he held out his arm and she nestled into his side, resting her head on his shoulder.

He regretted what they'd done, she knew that much. Matthew had yet to succeed in getting anything past Tessa. She knew him too well, as he did her.

Only to be expected, with how close they'd always been.

So close she'd not thought twice about marrying him. To keep Matthew safe she'd have done anything he asked of her.

He would be safe, she vowed silently. No matter how many times he flew across the Channel, he'd always make it back. He had to, he was her Matthew and she loved him.

Of course she did.

That evening more than ever Tessa recoiled at the thought of walking back into Esme's house with no Matthew by her side. Her heart was heavy and her spirits low so that walking at all took every last shred of energy she could muster.

Once Matthew had gone some way to absolving his conscience, they'd managed a pleasant enough day together, but it had felt different somehow.

Until now the time they'd spent together had been effortless but today she'd found herself watching every word and acutely aware of herself in his presence.

Not shy, she could never be shy with Matthew, but guarded, anxious that neither of them said or did anything else that got in the way of these few precious hours that were all they had.

Try as she might she'd not seen why it mattered so much to him that they'd married under what he clearly deemed to be false pretences. If there'd been no real need after all; and thinking about it she could see his point that as long as men were fighting a war and needing uniforms to fight in, her skills as a machinist at Ambrose's would never be surplus to requirements; then maybe they'd been a bit hasty in tying the knot, but she'd not love him any more or any less either way.

Only when Matthew had compared their marriage with Lil and Bertie's had it fallen short. To Tessa it felt as though he'd taken pure gold and bemoaned the fact it wasn't a diamond.

Briefly they'd returned to Esme's house so Matthew could change into his uniform and pick up his kitbag before they left to walk to the station, and Tessa had shown him the little muslin pouch she'd sewn to hold their lucky penny, and the stack of every one of his letters she kept along with it.

'Never, ever tell me I don't love the bones of you,' she'd told him shakily, and he'd held her tightly for a long moment before he'd released her abruptly to go and say his farewells to Hilary aild Esme.

Tessa had feared he'd no more want her there when he got on the train than he had when he'd gone back after Christmas, and determined as she was to be there this time, she'd been ready to stand her ground.

But Matthew had said nothing to discourage her. If anything he'd seemed to want her there. She'd considered the possibility that it might be easier for him to see her growing smaller from the train window since he'd professed their marriage to be not worth the paper it was written on, but she'd dismissed it again sharply, berating herself for thinking it in the first place.

It would never be easy for her and Matthew to be parted from each other.

★   ★   ★

On the platform he'd held her tightly once more and she'd felt him tremble.

This time he was going back to fly and. in case that meant he'd not see out this war he wanted every last moment with her.

'I love you,' he'd said, his voice choked. 'Tess, I love you.'

'I love you too,' she'd replied softly, but

he'd gazed sadly at her and the unspoken rebuke 'not proper, you don't' had hung in the air between them as it had since he'd uttered the very words hours earlier.

She felt so desolate she'd barely. the energy to lift her feet as she trudged along the side passageway and round to the back of Esme' s house.

She didn't want to walk back in there without Matthew, but for the life of her she couldn't think where else to be.

'Tess. Over here.'

Mindful of alerting Esme, Hilary kept her voice low as she called to her from where she was pegging out washing at the far end of the garden and relieved of the immediate necessity to walk back into the house where Matthew should be, Tessa turned and crossed the grass towards her.

At first she avoided Hilary's eyes, stooping to gather an armful of damp clothes from the basket which she draped over her arm before reaching for a handful of dolly pegs, for the moment at least keeping her thoughts to herself as 'She and Hilary worked side by side.

Only when the basket had been emptied did Hilary manage to catch her eye.

'Matthew get off all right?' she enquired quietly, and Tessa nodded.

'Packed off back to Norfolk and the cockpit of a bomber.'

To her own ears she sounded cold and bitter, and when Hilary started in surprise, it occurred to her that Matthew had told no-one but her that he was destined to fly into battle.

'I'd a notion something wasn't quite right,' Hilary stated. 'Not like you to be this distracted, Tess.'

Her eyes prickling with the threat of tears, Tessa gazed at her sadly.

'He's terrified he'll not last out this war, Hillie, and so am I. I'm so frightened I'll lose my Matthew, and we've not even had two full days, not time enough to say even half of it ...'

She broke off suddenly, seeing her own tears reflected in Hilary's eyes. 'I'm sorry, Hillie. You'll not be wanting to hear this, not with your Leo out there, too.'

Hilary smiled bravely, her hand resting on Tessa's arm in a gesture of solidarity.

'There's always more to say, Tess. No matter if you've weeks together, the minute you're alone again you'll think of a hundred things you should have said. Trick is to make sure you've not left out the most important bits.'

'Matthew knows how precious he is to me,' Tessa murmured, but Hilary looked at her pointedly.

'Does he? More to the point, do you?'

Tessa blinked at her in surprise. What was she getting at? She'd have had to have brought the pair of them up with her eyes shut to not know they thought the world of each other.

'Don't make my mistakes, Tess,' Hilary continued, keeping her voice low even though they both knew there was little chance Esme would haul herself up and out of her armchair.

'From the day he started courting me my Lee's had to put up with playing second fiddle to Ma. Had I consented to finding a place of our own he'd have had our names down on that list and he'd have been chuffed to bits about it.' Her voice caught and she took a deep breath to steady it. 'But I'd not do it, I'd not put him and our daughter first, and now she's happier under Granny Peg's roof and if Leo ... if that's the last I've seen of him, he'll have died thinking I never loved him enough.'

'Leo knows you love him,' Tessa protested. 'He knows as well, same as we all do, that you've looked after your ma for most of your life and you can't just up and leave her.'

Hilary shook her head sadly. 'She had a time of it, Tess. When Pa came back from the Great War, and his chest the worse for it, only a matter of months it was before they'd not let him back driving them buses and then he'd nothing to perk him up, see. Took it out on Ma for the rest of his days, he did. Always finding fault — she'd not put a foot right in Arthur Lane's opinion.'

'You'd not know it to hear her speak of him,' Tessa commented wryly. 'That's why you've been so loyal to her ever since then.'

Hilary nodded. 'Easier for her to remember him as the Arthur she married before the war left him a bitter and angry shell. You and Matthew weren't much more than babbies — if you'd picked up on it you'd have no lasting memory of it, but I remember it well enough, and I've let it tie me to Ma's side ever since.'

'Not your place to account for your pa's mistakes,' Tessa ventured softly.

'As comfortable as you've made life for Esme ...'

'At the expense of others,' Hilary interjected quietly. 'Victoria prefers to be billeted with a stranger than live under a roof where's she to mind her tongue with every word she utters in Granny's presence, and if Leo's not coming home; he'll never know that being without him all this time has made me see it how it is, that all these years I've mopped up after Ma's marriage and neglected my own to do it. He'll never know I've my heart set on walking out this house with him the minute he walks back into it.'

She clasped Tessa's shoulders with surprising strength and looked straight at her out of eyes that were a mirror of Matthew's.

'Don't waste a moment, Tess. Not when you've no idea how many you've got left.' She smiled sadly. 'Tell him. Tell my brother he means the world to you, and more besides. You think I've not noticed?' she added, seeing Tessa's stunned expression. 'Dragged up the pair of you, didn't I?

'I'd a notion Matthew thought more of you than he was letting on, and as for you, Tessa Lane, I know a woman in love when I see one!'

Tessa waited until much later, when both Esme and Hilary had retired to bed, and she was sitting at the table in darkness save the gentle glow of the candle, before she started to write. It would only be a short letter but it said all she needed to say.

Dear Matthew. I love you — proper.
Yours forever,
Tess.

A Plan Emerges

With no wish to be waylaid into small talk with anyone, Tessa kept her head bowed and her eyes averted from the usual Saturday afternoon crowd milling about the Bull Ring as she skirted the worst of it on her way to meet Lil at Green's Cafe.

She'd felt much the same this past week; unwilling to pass the time of day with folk at the factory — even Dorrie Cooper had quickly seen it was best to leave her be.

Lil would not have been discouraged quite so easily, but then Lil had spent the past week honeymooning in nearby Kenilworth with Bertie, so Tessa had been left to work at her machine, on automaton it felt like, with just her thoughts for company.

Come the end of each shift, she'd been first out of the gates and back under Esme's roof before the rest of them had so much as got their coats on.

Gone were the days she'd chosen to take a longer route through the park rather than hurry back to a house without Matthew. Waiting for his reply to her letter, every moment it took her to reach the house was a moment too long.

'Pair of you at it now, then,' Esme had commented the first evening Tessa had flown back through the doot and fell on the letters propped up on the mantel

'Hillie near enough knocking the postie off his feet one end of the day and you pouncing on them letters the other when there's some ofus been waiting on a pot of tea these past three hours or more ...'

She'd not queried it though, Tessa noticed. Given that Esme made it her business to know all that went on under her roof, she was surprisingly dismissive of how suddenly desperate her daughter-in-law was to hear from Matthew.

It might have been down to Hilary filling her in, though if she'd said anything, Esme would have had plenty to say in return.

More likely, Tessa surmised grimly, that the old lady had her suspicions and was for once keeping them to herself in the vain hope that whatever fleeting fancy *Lady Muck* had for her Mattie, it would all blow over by this time next week.

She'd have to lump it then, wouldn't she? Tessa knew she'd never been thought good enough for Matthew, by his ma in any case, but she'd not let it bother her thus far — she'd not start heeding Esme's, ramblings now.

Matthew loved her, she knew he did. He'd been trying to tell her that day they'd spent together up on the Lickeys, when he'd pointed out that they'd not married for the right reasons, that she didn't love him that way.

Not once had he argued the same for himself. At the station, he'd made a last attempt to tell her — he had told her but she'd not understood, and the defeated look in his eyes Tessa saw again every time she closed hers.

He'd be thinking he'd made a mistake telling her, that she didn't feel the same way he did. How could she not? Together they'd grown up and grown closer. There'd not be anyone else for either of them. She could see that now.

Once Matthew received her letter, he'd write back the first chance he got. He'd not keep her waiting, not over this.

But he'd have had it in his hand a week since and she'd yet to hear from him.

The only post she'd received was a postcard from Lil and Bertie, with a postscript tagged on the end from Lil saying they'd be back on Saturday and asking to meet up with Tessa at Green's once her shift had finished.

She'd received nothing from Matthew.

They'd heard on the wireless that the East Coast had been getting a bit of a pasting so he'd likely not have had a moment to himself to write back to her.

He'd know how she felt now at least, so it would bolster his spirits a little, but even this was a small comfort to Tessa as she flew back through the door night after night to find that the postman had yet again brought nothing from Matthew.

She'd been all set to run home briefly to check if today was any different, but to do so would have made her late meeting Lil. In any case, if yet again she'd be met with further disappointment, she'd be as well putting it back a few hours.

As it was, she arrived outside Green's with a moment or two to spare, where she waited for a good ten more before Lil finally appeared, full of apologies for keeping her waiting.

'I called in to see Ginny Cirelli,' she explained, ushering Tessa before her into the cafe. 'I'd plenty of time when I left Dorrie's, but Ginny had a fair bit she needed to get off her chest and I didn't like to rush off before she'd done. I'm sorry, Tess.'

Tessa waved away her apology. 'Not like I've been stood out there half the afternoon, is it? You're here now anyway, and no doubt you're bursting to fill me in on the joys of Kenilworth so am I right in thinking we'd be best off ordering a large pot of tea?'

It would be a relief to have something else to think about for five minutes, a distraction from the state of constant jitters she was in waiting for Matthew's reply to drop through the letterbox.

Tea poured and cakes chosen, they found a table by the window, Lil quiet for a moment as she stirred sugar into her tea, no sign of the excited ten to the dozen chattering Tessa had expected.

With the stop off she'd made on the way into town, Tessa suspected she might have a fair idea what had left Lil so distracted.

'How is Ginny?' she asked her. 'Are they still holding Alec?'

Lil looked up at her. 'They've still got him under lock and key,' she said tersely. 'Ginny's about how you'd expect, Tess. Been down that police station every day, much good it's done her. They're on about shipping Alec and a good few others off somewhere else, but they'll not tell her where.'

'I should've been to see her,' Tessa

murmured. 'With you not here ... '

She'd not thought about it until now. Not that she and Ginny were friends as such; were it not for Lil's presence under the Cirellis' roof their paths might never have crossed; but after the many afternoons Tessa had spent by the fire in their front room poring over dress measurements with Lil, she could at least claim to have a passing acquaintance with Ginny.

Would it have hurt her to have dropped by at least once to see how she was holding up? With Lil away, it would have been the decent thing to do.

But her mind had been so full of Matthew she'd literally given no-one else a moment's thought.

'Not your worry, Tess,' Lil replied matter-of-factly. 'She's friends in the Italian quarter in any case, and more of them than not in the same boat.'

She smiled sadly. 'She'll not give up on her Alec, I know that much. White as snow her face was the entire time we were talking, and shadows under her eyes like she'd not slept in months, but every so often she'd perk up arid tell me how, when he's freed, they'll be leaving here and finding a little cottage to rent in the countryside, where folk won't give them a wide berth and whisper behind their backs.'

'Keeping her going, I expect,' Tessa sighed, and Lil nodded.

'She even offered me and Bertie first refusal on renting the house in Hockley Street.'

'What, all three floors of it? Set you back a pretty penny that would, I imagine.' Catching the spark of interest in Lil's tone, Tessa eyed her curiously.

'Or are you after keeping the business ticking over for her as well?'

Lil raised an eyebrow at her. 'I'm no landlady. I've enough trouble looking after myself, let alone a whole house full of tenants.'

'You've done all right for yourself. Not been here a year yet and you're as much a part of Brum as Bertie's piano.'

'Jury's out on which of us he treasures most.' Lil smiled fondly, but her thoughts were still with Ginny Cirelli. 'For Ginny's sake more than mine I hope she gets to pack her bags and waltz off into the sunset.'

'But you think there's a chance she won't.'

Lil stared into her tea. 'I hope she will, but the longer he's locked up, Tess … '

'I know. Police won't be falling over themselves to exonerate Alec Cirelli though, will they? Might take a while; but we'll just have to keep faith he'll be out eventually.' Tessa watched her thoughtfully. 'You're thinking about renting their house, aren't you?'

'I'd have to talk it over with Bertie,' Lil mused. 'We'd decided to put our names down for a house anyway. You know I love the bones of Dorrie Cooper, but that flat's barely big enough for her.'

'Only right you'd want your own place anyway,' Tessa conceded, her thoughts turning to Leo and Hilary, and the similar chance they'd passed up, and for what? 'But will she not want the boarding house run as usual?'

Lil shook her head. 'Long as we pay her the rent so she can pay hers in turn, what we do with the place would be our concern. She's no thought to coming back here, Tess.'

'But what else would you do with it?'

Talking of Alec Cirelli' s release as if it were a certainty when as yet it was anything but, seemed a little premature, but Tessa could see how it cheered Lil to be doing so, so said nothing at all.

Just back from her honeymoon, her spirits should be soaring no matter what — if.it brought the smile back to her face Tessa was only too happy to encourage her to share the thoughts she'd clearly been having about the possible future of the house on Hockley Street.

With a great sense of purpose Lil leaned forwards in her chair, the light in her eyes indicative of the ideas lurking behind them.

'You're to hear me out, Tessa Lane, before you utter so much as a word, all right?' She paused for Tessa to nod before she continued. 'That house, it's far too big to have just me and Bertie rattling around in it, and chances are even with his wage and mine we'd be pushed to find the rent.

'Thing is, we'd only need one floor, wouldn't we, so say we took the top one, then you and Matthew could have the second one ... Tessa, you promised you'd not interrupt ... which just leaves the ground floor that in my humble opinion is prime pickings for Birmingham' s premier dressmaking establishment run by you, of course, with me as your willing second in command. What do you think?'

Tessa shook her head firmly. 'I think that will take capital I don't have, Lil, which I've a vague recollection of pointing out to you once before.'

'You might not have it,' Lil ventured cautiously. 'But I have. You know how my Aunty Marianne hit the big time with her singing — every penny she saved she left to me. Chances are I've enough to buy that house outright if Ginny's of a mind to sell it. Furnishing and stocking a shop I can certainly stretch to.'

Bewildered, Tessa stared at her. 'But if you've had money all along why on earth do you slog away at Ambrose's?' she managed eventually.

Lil sunk her fork into her custard slice, sending it crumbling all over her plate.

'You know why, Tess. I wanted to make my own way in the world. Aside from the cheek I'd have to be living off Aunty Mai's earnings when I'd left my gran with no hope of me ever singing a note, I've no right to expect such an easy ride of things, nor would I want it.'

'So what's changed?'

Lil looked at her as if the answer was obvious. 'We'd not be frittering it away and seeing nothing in return, would we? We'd be using it to set ourselves up in business and the flair you have with a needle and thread, chances are it'd not take us all that long to replace it, with interest on top I shouldn't wonder.' She smiled sadly. 'Perhaps Gran will see her way to being proud of me for something other than belting out show tunes in feathers and sequins.'

'Way you told it, she'd have no bones to pick so long as you were well and happy.'

Tessa was struggling to order her thoughts. 'As you've every right to be, seeing as it's your money, Lil I've no claim to it, you know that.'

'I've no dressmaking business without you,' Lil returned bluntly. 'You're the talent, Tess. I'd just be putting up the initial outlay. We'd make it back soon enough and beyond that it'd have both our names on it.'

Tessa shook her head numbly. 'It's too much, Lil. You've known me five minutes.'

'Since the moment I stepped off that train with no earthly idea where I was going,' Lil recalled. 'Not only did you direct me to the warmest welcome in the whole city courtesy of Ginny Cirelli, you took me under your wing at Ambrose's. Were it not for you, I'd not have met my Bertie. Tessa you've been more of a friend in these past months than some folk would manage in a lifetime.'

'You'd have got by all right,' Tessa mumbled. 'If you'd not bumped into me you'd have accosted someone else.'

Lil beamed at her. 'True. Picked you, though, didn't I? And I think it's fair to say I'd not have the life I have now if I hadn't.'

'Even so, I've no right to be profiting from your Aunty Marianne's singing career,' Tessa protested, and the smile faded as Lil looked very seriously at her.

'If she were here, she'd be right behind us, Tess. In a way she did the same, didn't she? Going off to London to seek her fortune. She could sing, there's none would argue with that — she'd only to open her mouth — but fame can be fickle and the way she told it singers like her were ten a penny down there. She'd no guarantee of making it, but she tried nonetheless. Top up?'

Lil lifted the teapot to refill their cups. 'I'm not getting ahead of myself, Tess. As yet I know there's a chance, as much as I hope and pray otherwise, that Ginny might not be going anywhere, but if she and Alec do get their happy ending, I just think we'd be as well getting ours too so some more good can come out of all this.'

Tessa sipped her tea thoughtfully. 'Well, when you put it like that.'

'I notice you've not protested half as much at the thought of having a place of your own with Matthew,' Lil added, a knowing gleam in her eyes. 'That'll be down to you thinking of him as your closest friend and nothing more, will it? You know, I might have almost believed you had I not seen the two of your heads together at our wedding.'

'All right, Mrs Cooper,' Tessa interjected, but she couldn't quite halt the smile. 'You've made your point.'

'Which you've not disputed,' Lil noted gleefully. 'Bertie's said as much all along, you know.'

'Yes, well, your Bertie has far too much to say for himself.' Tessa smiled at her over the rim of her cup. 'But yes, Lil, I love Matthew every bit as much as you love Bertie. There, I've admitted it. Happy now?'

'Not half as much as Matthew' will be, I reckon,' Lil declared brightly, reaching for her purse. 'Right then, if I'm to regale you with the delights of our week in the wilds of Warwickshire, I think we could do with another custard slice!'

★ ★ ★

An afternoon with Lil had lifted her spirits, Tessa reflected as she walked home later, and not just because of the possible opportunity to earn a living as a dressmaker she'd so unexpectedly tossed into her lap.

She couldn't claim to be indifferent to the prospect, but it was Lil's company she'd enjoyed, Lil's exuberant presence she'd missed over the past week they could have talked about nothing more than the weather and she knew she'd have come away from Green's feeling just as she did now.

In Lillian Cooper's company it was

impossible to feel despondent for long. Truth to tell, she'd more right than Tessa to admit defeat, given the grief she'd gone through following the death of first her mother then her Aunty Marianne, but she'd picked herself up, dusted herself off and found the courage to begin a new life from scratch.

Her worry over the Cirellis was the one shadow passing intennittently across Lil's face but she'd even found a positive outcome to that.

Not that Tessa had given up hope in comparison; she refused to contemplate anything other than Matthew's safe return once this war had run its course; but waiting to hear from him this past week, while hearing reports of bombings along the East Coast, had taken its toll.

Listening to Lil make plans as if there was no reason at all why the war should alter them, Tessa had found it easier to believe it wouldn't.

She'd been fretting over nothing, she chided herself as she walked round to the back door of Esme's house.

Each and every letter Matthew wrote to her she'd treasured from the start, but if he'd no time to write another she'd know he loved her — she didn't need the postman to tell her that.

'Had your fill of dashing home like the wind then, have you?' Esme exclaimed the second Tessa walked in. 'If you'd a bit more patience instead of giving up and going off gallivanting, you'd have had news of my boy hours ago.'

He'd written! At last Matthew had written to her. Shaking like a leaf suddenly, Tessa dived towards the mantel, snatching up the envelope bearing Matthew's familiar scrawl.

She'd waited so long for this she didn't at first notice anything amiss. Only when she sank into a chair, her legs too weak to carry her any further away from Esme's interfering presence, did she realise the envelope had already been opened.

She looked up sharply at the old lady. It had to have been her! Hilary would never do such a thing!

'You've no right opening my letters!'

Esme stared evenly back at her. 'My girl, you'd be wise taking a closer look at that there envelope before you go accusing me of owt.'

Turning it over, Tessa focused on the letters that blurred and swam. In her haste she'd seen only Matthew's writing — if he'd addressed it to the erstwhile snowman in the garden chances are she'd not have noticed.

As it was, he'd addressed it to *The Lane Family*. Not as with every other previous letter, to Tessa only.

A cold dread gripped her as she drew the letter out and with shaking fingers unfolded it to read the brief note he'd written.

Got my wings. Am safe. Matthew.

There had to be another letter, addressed just to her. It was the only explanation. But even as she searched in vain along the mantel, Tessa knew there wasn't.

With him flying now, he'd clearly had no more than a spare minute to scribble a few words, but why send them to his

207

mother when in as many words he could have written briefly to Tessa? I love you, too — if that's all he'd had time to tell her then that's all she'd have needed to read.

But she'd not be reading it because he'd not be writing it. The truth settled heavily over her.

In the same way she'd vowed never to write a word rather than send anything that might distress him, Matthew would from now on be redirecting his letters to the family as a whole, thus letting Tessa know he was safe without having to write the words that would break her heart.

Somehow, when she knew Matthew as she knew herself, she'd, got it wrong.

He didn't love her.

She couldn't think of moving into Hockley Street now. Chances are it'd not be that simple anyway. Alec and Ginny would need to get their happy ending first, when happy endings hereabouts seemed to have been rationed along with everything else.

Lil and Bertie had stumbled across

theirs nonetheless, but then Lil was due a bit of luck after the life she'd had. If just one of them was to come up smiling, only right it should be her.

Same could be said for Hilary, mind. After a lifetime of running round after Esme Lane, a happy ending was the least she deserved, but as the days turned into weeks and the pockets of soldiers returning from the beaches of Dunkirk became fewer and farther between, the hope she clung to that Leo would be returned to her in one piece was slipping through her fingers.

Not surprising then that she was dismissive of Tessa's quiet distress following Matthew's letter.

'You know he's safe, Tess,' she pointed out, her tone distinctly frosty. 'More than can be said for some of us.'

Put like that, she'd no right to feel sorry for herself, Tessa conceded.

However hard it was for her to come to terms with Matthew's rejection of her, she was at least spared the worry of not knowing if he was alive or dead.

He continued to write with as much regularity as he'd done before, the one difference being the name he scribbled on the envelope.

As part of the Lane family whether Esme liked it or not, Tessa had every right to read Matthew's letters and did so the minute she returned from work to find one propped up on the mantel.

To his ma and Hilary he naturally wrote a lot less freely and though she'd not expect otherwise, Tessa missed the way he'd once written to her, the warm and easy tone that had made her feel as if he were there with her and not miles away on an air base in Norfolk

But if she was left feeling shut out from his thoughts like she'd never once been until now, she at least knew he was safe.

Not quite so easy to be philosophical though when she was around Lil and Bertie. Unable to bear the knowing winks they shared if Matthew's name cropped up, Tessa enlightened the pair of them and no more was said, but as much as she treasured them both, just being in their company when they had everything she'd lost felt so incredibly hard.

Casting around for a distraction, she allowed Hilary to coerce her into enrolling with the Women's Voluntary Service.

'Half of Brum treat the clothing exchange like a communal rag bag,' she complained. 'Bit of darning here and there is all most of it needs. You can spare an evening or two a week, can't you, Tess?'

She'd spare every one of them rather than sit at home with Esme's silent gloating or have to see Bertie looking at Lil like she was the world and more.

Darning, patching, remodelling — she'd time for all of it since she'd no more letters to write.

'You're a treasure, Tess,' the women at the WVS never seemed to grow tired of telling her. 'Our own Mrs Sew and Sew.'

Whether she was sewing on missing buttons, reinforcing threadbare blankets with flannelette, or in the case of jumpers seemingly beyond repair, unpicking the wool and winding it around a bottle of hot water to leave her with wool that was almost as good as new and could be knitted into something else, Tessa's evenings were taken up with her new duties at the town hall.

Time was she'd have enjoyed herself, but the ease with which her needle flew in and out left her mind free to wander, and always it settled on Matthew.

Of course it did. Hadn't she kept him in her thoughts constantly since he'd gone off to join up last year? She'd do it still.

If nothing else, he remained her dearest friend and she wanted, him kept safe, to which end she'd not taken her ring off, nor had she any intention of doing so, not when she'd believed this whole time that as long as she wore it, he'd be returned to her safely.

Maybe she was foolish still to believe it'd make a difference either way but with reports on the wireless every day of airborne battles, she'd not be taking any chances.

He'd done his bit to defend the East Coast and now, as the South Coast came under fire, with daily attacks on ports and airfields, he wrote a brief note to inform them he was being posted to a base in Dover. It seemed to Tessa that wherever this war went, Matthew was ordered to follow.

But he'd see the end of it. As long as she wore his ring and kept their lucky penny stowed away with the letters she'd not part with no matter how much it hurt to read them now, he'd be all right. Nothing would happen to Matthew.

When the telegram arrived, it was Hilary whose world crumbled around her.

Since the first lot of soldiers had returned back in May, she'd clung to a waning hope that Leo would eventually turn up amongst them, but it was August now and the knock on the door was not her husband too weary to turn his key but the postman who held in his hand the news she'd known she had coming.

Leo had been killed in action.

A Shock Discovery

Rising a little earlier than usual the following morning, Tessa padded softly
down the stairs. Such stealth had long
been necessary if she was to avoid dis-
turbing Esme and therefore manage a
cup of tea in peace before she left to walk
to work, but today she'd another more
important reason to tiptoe so gingerly
around the floorboards she knew would
creak from even the lightest tread.

Muffled sobs through the wall had
kept her awake long into the small hours
but she'd woken to find a blanket of subdued silence had settled over the house.

If Hilary had at last slipped into the
oblivion of sleep, Tessa was determined
she'd not disturb her. Used to her Hillie
being up at the crack of dawn and ready
with the pot on to boil, Esme would
be clamouring for her attention soon
enough.

To this end Tessa had risen with a few

extra minutes to spare. She couldn't leave the pot on the gas, of course, but she'd at least have it filled and fresh tea leaves in the strainer. Not that Esme would ever think of fending for herself for a change, but when Hilary was summoned, at least there'd be a little less for her to do.

Slipping quietly into the unlit back room, Tessa was startled by the figure sitting stiffly at the table.

Hilary was not, as she'd thought, asleep in her bed, but up and dressed, the paleness of her face and the shadows under her eyes eerie in the gloom of early morning seeming to suggest she'd not slept at all.

'Hillie?' Tessa exclaimed softly, but as she stepped towards her, Hilary rose from her chair, and it was then that Tessa noticed she had her coat on and buttoned, and the beret she wore for outings perched on her curls.

'I'm going to Wales,' Hilary whispered 'I need to be with Victoria.'

'Of course you do,' Tessa agreed gently. 'Take as long as you need, Hillie. I'll

215

keep things ticking over here …'

'Shush!' Hilary stood stock stiff suddenly, gripping Tessa's arm as she strained to listen, but as yet there was no noise from the front room.

'You know she'll not be up yet,' Tessa attempted to reassure her, but Hilary was already darting towards the back door, where her suitcase stood packed and waiting.

Seeing the way she struggled to lift it, the truth dawned on Tessa long before her sister-in-law managed one last troubled glance over her shoulder.

This was no short respite while she adjusted to losing Leo. She'd crammed everything she owned into that suitcase and once she'd dragged it to New Street, she'd be buying a one way ticket.

Hilary had no intention of coming back.

★ ★ ★

'That'll have knocked Esme well and truly for six then,' Lil sighed later, when

Tessa confided in her over their lunch break. 'I know your Hillie's frayed the apron strings just lately but she'll not have expected her to snip them completely, will she?'

'None of us did,' Tessa replied flatly. 'Only to be expected she'd want to be with Victoria at a time like this; but I'd not thought for a minute she'd turn her back on her ma for good.'

'Perhaps she won't,' Lil suggested. 'Might be the grief talking, Tess. Once she's had time to adjust and she's thinking clearly again, chances are she'll land back on the doorstep.'

'Reckon Esme'll have me packing her off on the next train to Wales if not,'

Tessa sighed. 'She were none too pleased when I dared to wake her up this morning, but she'd not have had so much as a cup of tea until tonight if I'd just left her.'

'Right shock it'd have been as well, waking up to find herself alone in the house,' Lil pointed out. 'Thought Hilary might have hung on a bit to tell her she was off, instead of sneaking out like that.'

'She couldn't,' Tessa said bluntly. 'Look on her face when she thought she'd heard Esme stir — she was out that door like a rabbit.' She pushed her half-eaten dinner away. 'Yours truly left to break the news,'

To her own ears she sounded bitter, for which she felt instantly ashamed, Hilary had raised her and cared for her when she'd been little more than a child herself.

Consumed with grief now, and likely not thinking straight at all, she'd every right to leave Tessa to hold everything together for her.

She owed Hillie that much.

But it wasn't Hillie she'd been left with, was it? As far back as she could remember, there'd not been a moment when Esme had regarded her as any-thing more than an inconvenience, an extra mouth to feed.

Even now, with Tessa reliant on no-one but herself, the most she'd come to expect from Esme was a scornful contempt that more often than not she made no attempt to curb.

This very morning she'd responded to the news of Hilary' s departure with yet more of the same. Not that Tessa had been naive enough to expect gratitude that she'd thought to boil a fresh pot and make her some breakfast, but all she'd got instead was indignation that she'd woken her up at such an unearthly hour.

'Unless you're of a mind to make your own tea from now on, you'd best get used to it,' Tessa had responded tartly, but inside she'd been despairing as ahead of her she saw an endless round of battles with Esme.

She'd been left to run around after her, and she wasn't even her own daughter.

Lil placed a hand over hers. 'Will you let Matthew know, Tess?'

'There's no need,' she replied quickly. 'Nothing he can do, is there? He's got enough to worry about in any case.'

'Do you not think he might want to know all the same?' Lil ventured cautiously. 'Hillie's his sister, for a start.'

Tessa shook her head firmly ... No. I'll not give him anything else to worry about.'

'He'll worry about you anyway, Tess,' Lil told her quietly. 'You'll not stop him doing that. Easy to see he treasures you, even if you've not got what me and Bertie have got, though I'm not convinced you haven't,' she added. 'No matter what you say. Write to him, Tess.'

'So I can reply to all the letters he writes to me?' Tessa demanded bitterly. 'If he's got nothing to say, then neither have I.'

Lil sighed, shaking her head. 'Stubborn as mules, the pair of you. Well, you'll have to write to him when you move into Hockley Street. You can't not give him your new address.'

'I told you, I'm not moving anywhere,' Tessa stated firmly. 'Hockley Street's your happy ending, Lil, not mine.'

'No reason why it can't be both,' Lil argued. 'I know you're not of a mind to live there without Matthew, not when that's how we planned it, but there's still the shop, Tess. Without you I've no hope of making a proper go of it.' She smiled ruefully. 'You might as well give it a try. For one thing, if you're right and Matthew regrets putting that ring on your finger, you've nothing to lose by moving on with your life, have you?'

'All very well moving on,' Tessa sighed. 'While I've got Esme to think of, moving out's a different matter.'

It was all pie in the sky anyway, she thought. Hockley Street and Birmingham's premier dressmaking establishment, as Lil had grandly referred to it, as yet remained a boarding house and, more importantly, Ginny Cirelli's home.

No harm in Lil thinking positive, of course, but there was no sense in talking of it as though it was a certainty when Alec was still being investigated.

'Not happening yet anyway, is it?' she ventured cautiously. Not for one minute would she trample over Lil's dreams, but then neither did she want her to get her hopes up.

'That's where you're wrong,' Lil replied quietly, but all the same she attempted to quell the beginnings of a smile. 'I'm sorry, Tess. I've tried to keep this to myself. Hardly seems proper for me to be celebrating with what's happened to your Hilary.'

'Seems to me that's even more reason why you should,' Tessa countered.

'We could do with something to smile about.' She eyed her curiously. 'Has Alec been freed?'

Lil nodded, finally allowing the smile to widen. 'He's back home with Ginny as of yesterday afternoon. Pair of them were on Dorrie's doorstep last night wanting to know if Bertie and me have given any thought to taking the house.'

'Blimey,' Tessa exclaimed. 'They're keen to be off, then.'

'Nothing to stay for,' Lil said simply. 'Way they see it, they've wasted enough time. Alec's got a sister who lives out Derbyshire way — she's got a farm in the Dales. They're going to her while they look for their own place.'

'Ginny must be so incredibly relieved,' Tessa murmured, and Lil placed a hand over hers.

'When it's meant to be, this war makes no odds. Matthew will come home, Tess. Make a go of the business with me and you'll be set for the rest of your lives you'll have together.'

Far more likely she'd end up with one failed marriage behind her and seeking solace in her dressmaking, Tessa thought, but either way she'd nothing to lose by setting up the business with Lil.

Moving in above the premises she'd not be able to do, not while she had Esme to look after, but she could work there all the same. Ambrose's, Hockley Street — where was the difference?

If she was to keep Esme in tea leaves, she had to work somewhere, and if the old lady took offence at being left with her own company all day, she'd just have to lump it. Not as if they were rolling in money and Tessa could afford to stay at home and run around after her all day long.

'My name's not Hilary,' Tessa muttered to herself as, with a heavy heart, she steeled herself to walk back through the door that evening.

Though in fairness to Hilary, since she'd taken up with the Women's Voluntary Service, the days she'd been at liberty to run around after her ma from dawn til dusk had been few and far between.

Tessa was due at the Town Hall herself for a couple of hours after tea. Just this once though, she was considering making her excuses. With Hilary gone only a matter of hours, Esme would still be reeling from the shock. Not that she'd appreciate Tessa sitting in with her all evening, but it seemed the decent thing to do nonetheless.

She'd wait and suss Esme's frame of mind once she'd had her tea, Tessa decided, as she finally steeled herself to turn the door handle.

'Decided to come in then, have you?' Esme demanded frostily. 'Loitering out there like you've owt more pressing to see to than my tea!'

'I'll have the spuds chopped and on to boil in a jiffy,' Tessa sighed, gritting her teeth against the wave of exhaustion that had her feeling as limp as a wet rag the second she'd stepped back over the threshold. 'Tea won't be long, Esme.'

'Be a fair bit quicker if my Hillie were here to do the honours,' Esme retorted bluntly. 'Looks like I'll have to make do with you til she gets back, don't it?'

She settled back in her armchair, pulling her shawl tightly around her. 'Fire wants stoking before you get started on them spuds.'

She'd not shatter the old lady's illusions by voicing her suspicions that *her Hillie* might have cooked their tea for the last time, Tessa thought grimly as she poked at the dying embers of the fire.

Nor would she point out that it was the middle of August and hot enough outside that they'd no need of a fire in the grate, even if Esme's chest gave her twice as much trouble.

For the sake of a quiet life it was simpler just to get on with it.

'Like middle of winter in this house,' Esme continued. 'Can't say as I blame my Hillie taking herself off to the country for a bit of sun. She'll have timed it right and all, with schools shutting up for the summer — week or two with our Vic and she'll be right as rain.'

With the fire revived and crackling slowly back to life, Tessa replaced the poker and got stiffly to her feet.

'Best place for her to be,' she agreed. 'Last of that bacon do you for tea? Think we've some cauliflower left as well ... '

'Sits heavy on my stomach, that does,' Esme protested. 'And that bacon's far too salty — irritates my chest. Just scramble me some eggs and mash them spuds up with them. Meantime a pot of tea would go down a treat, seeing as I'm having to wait a bit longer than I'm used to,' she added, as Tessa disappeared into the kitchen.

She'd no hope of passing muster as Hilary's replacement, had she? She could whip up three course banquets every day and in Esme's eyes she'd not be half as good.

In truth, Hilary's WVS commitments more often than not had her coming in at this hour, and later still, Esme's tea on the table as and when she'd got round to it, but the many times Esme had grumbled would have fallen clean out of her head, Tessa realised.

In her absence Hilary would be taking on the makings of a saint and in comparison with Tessa's second-rate efforts her praises sung at every conceivable opportunity.

That was one decision she'd not be agonising over then, Tessa vowed to herself as she lowered the chopped up potatoes into the pan. Once tea was over and done with; she'd stop long enough to make sure Esme was tucked up warm then she'd be off to the Town Hall.

'Lil told me how your Hilary's had the telegram,' Dorrie Cooper said quietly, as she and Tessa worked side by side to sort through a new batch of donations to the clothing exchange. 'All this time she's clung on, poor love. Still, it'll do her a bit of good to be with Victoria.' She glanced wryly at Tessa.

'Esme'll not be best pleased, I take it?'

'Hard pushed to tell what offends her most,' Tessa said flatly. 'Being deserted by Hilary or having to make do with me.'

'She's lucky she's got you,' Dorrie pointed out 'You never know, Tess. Might make her think again. All that fuss she made about you and Matthew getting wed, but she'd not have a daughter-in-law if you'd not, would she? You'd have nowt tying you to Esme Lane — you could be up and off the minute the fancy took you.'

Tessa shook her head slowly. 'I'd not do it, Dorrie. Married or not, I'll not turn my back just like that.' She picked up a threadbare towel, running her finger thoughtfully across the bits still intact. 'Reckon I can make a good half a dozen flannels out of this. Lil's told you about her plans for Hockley Street, then?'

'I might have heard about it once or

twice.' Dorrie smiled fondly. 'All she talks about, bless her. I'd a notion Bertie might have taken umbrage, but happen he's as fired up about it as she is.'

'You know Bertie,' Tessa stated. 'If Lil's happy, he'll not be far behind.'

Dorrie nodded. 'He's a good lad. Pair of them deserve a place of their own and I'll not stand in their way. Be strange though, Tess, being in that flat on my own. Nigh on twenty-two years I've had Bea and Bertie under my feet, and Lil for the past three months.' She chuckled to herself. 'Be so quiet without our Lil I'll be hearing pins drop all over the place.'

'They'll not abandon you, Dorrie,' Tessa assured her. 'You'll still see a fair bit of them.'

'I know,' Dorrie conceded. 'They've talked of me moving with them, but I'm not of a mind to pack up and leave my Bea's home, least not til she's back and packing up with me.' She paused, setting down the discarded cotton dress she'd been inspecting to look at Tessa. 'Time was you were thinking of moving into Hockley Street yourself. Be nice and handy once you've got the business up and running, wouldn't it?'

'But not so handy for running round after Esme morning and night,' Tessa retorted, eyeing her suspiciously. 'Has Lil been on at you to put a word in? I've told her — I'm more than happy to spend my days taking measurements and running up designs, but out of hours I've got Esme to think of.'

Dorrie smiled at her defiant tone. 'Lil's said nothing of the sort, Tess. This is me pointing out you've the talent to make a good go of it as a dressmaker and so much easier it'd be for you not to be running backwards and forwards all the time.'

'That's as maybe,' Tessa admitted. For now I've no choice. Until Esme shocks us all by fending for herself for a change, I can't walk out on her.'

'Like I said, she's lucky she's got you to look after her,' Dorrie declared bluntly. 'Might have put a roof over your head but she's not given you an easy time of it since, has she?'

Tessa shrugged, her eyes fixed on the intricately stitched silk lining of a grey woollen coat as with a practised eye she searched for any parts needing repair.

'Not for Esme's sake I'll keep things ticking over,' she said quietly. 'It's Hillie who deserves my loyalty. All Esme's done these past twenty-two years is remind me I'm no more than a lodger. Reckon she'd prefer a lodger, in fact — might make herself a bit more money out of it.'

She'd meant to keep her voice light, but she knew she'd sounded bitter.

'Oh, Tess.' Dorrie had been gathering up the relatively small amount of garments fit for the exchange with no need of Tessa's needle and thread, but she dropped them back onto the table and reached an arm around her shoulders. 'If she'll not think of you as part of her family, there's no-one else in it who'd agree with her. Look, how about we grab two minutes for a cuppa tea?'

Tessa nodded, managing a smile. 'I'll

just finish going over this coat.'

'Nice stitching, that.' Dorrie peered over her shoulder. 'Things folk give away — nowt wrong with it far as I can see. Right then, I'll get this tea poured, shall I?'

'I'll only be a minute,' Tessa promised, but the words were barely out of her mouth when she saw something that had her clutching Dorrie's sleeve.

'Whatever's the matter, Tess?'

'Look' With a shaking finger, she traced the letters of the name stitched so perfectly into the collar of the coat.

Tessa Thorne.

'Well, I'll be,' Dorrie exclaimed softly. 'What are the chances?'

Bewildered, Tessa stared at. She'd never seen this coat before in her life and yet it had her own name — the one she'd gone by before marrying Matthew anyway — stitched inside.

There had to be another Tessa Thorne living in the district. Not that she knew of any, and it was an unusual name, but it was the only explanation that made sense.

Dorrie had picked it up and was casting her own expert eye over the workmanship.

'Should have known,' she said, more to herself than to Tessa.

'Stitching of this quality you don't see every day. Definitely a Tessa Thorne original ... '

Tessa stared at her. 'This isn't my coat, Dorrie.'

'I know, love.' She smiled at her. 'It's your mother's, Tess.'

Her mother's coat. She'd spent the past five minutes holding her own mother's coat in her hands while she'd pored over every inch of the stitching.

Her mother, who'd been gone the best part of twenty-two years. Only months old when she'd died, Tessa recalled nothing of her — she'd not even seen a photograph. If Esme had ever had such a thing in her possession, she'd never said as much. Tessa couldn't even picture her own mother and yet in her hands she'd held her coat.

Maybe that too had once been in Esme's possession, but unprepared to fill up any of her tiny house with her dead neighbour's things, she'd have likely disposed of the lot as soon as she'd had chance.

All Tessa had of her mother was a lasting sadness, and a deep-rooted sense of blame. If Esme had got rid of the rest of it, she'd made sure to let Tessa know the very reason she'd ended up shoved under her roof.

'Yer own ma were that fond of you, she left you when you were no more than a babby!'

Tessa's mother had buried her husband but their daughter — the baby Tessa — should have given her enough of a reason to go on living. But she hadn't, and there'd not been a day since when Esme hadn't been ready to remind her of it.

Tessa's mother hadn't loved her enough to stay with her. It was Tessa's fault she'd died.

'Are you all right, Tess?' Dorrie was pressing a mug of tea into her hand.

'There you go, get that down you. Three sugars — good for shock. Never mind this rationing lark.'

Tessa looked up at her. 'She named me after herself.'

'She did, yes. Soon as she knew she were expecting you, she was convinyed she was having a girl, and she was determined you'd be Tessa, same as her.'

'She must have loved me, then,' Tessa whispered. 'To begin with, she must have done ... '

'Course she did!' Dorrie exclaimed. 'Nine months she talked of nowt else, and proud as punch she was when you were born, wheeling you out for all the world to see!' She put her arm around Tessa's shoulders. 'There's none would blame you for feeling like she turned her back on you, but you're not to think she didn't love you. It were the pain of losing your pa, see. She'd not looked after herself proper neither, all them years he'd been off fighting in the Great War — she'd weakened herself body and mind. So much so the doctor reckoned she'd no chance of seeing out her pregnancy but she were that chuffed to be having you, I reckon sheer spirit brought you into the world, Tess.'

'But she'd not enough of it left to keep herself alive,' Tessa said quietly.

'You knew my mother, then, Dorrie.'

'She were a good friend to me,' Dorrie declared. 'Pair of us used to sit in Green's and talk of getting a passage on a ship to Paris where we'd set up our own boutique.' She squeezed Tessa's shoulders. 'We were you and Lil thirty years ago.'

Tessa stroked the wool of her mother's coat, draped now over her lap. Her mother had made this coat herself. She'd designed it, stitched it, and harboured dreams of setting up her own business ... footsteps in which Tessa would follow thirty years later.

'Had a way with a needle and thread, your ma did,' Dorrie continued fondly.

'Chip off the old block, you are, Tess. Which is why I'll be the first to raise a glass to your future as a dressmaker. We didn't get as far as Paris, so it's down

236

to you, Tess. Take this chance to do what you've always wanted, and you'll be making your ma's dreams come true along with yours.'

A quiet word from Dorrie in the ear of the head woman at the Town Hall and Tessa was granted an early finish. Given a say in it she'd have preferred to work the rest of her shift rather than slink back home to Esme, but she'd no energy to argue.

Her mother's coat she held bundled up under her own as she walked slowly home. A clear sky overhead, there wasn't a drop of rain in sight, and if she happened to cross paths with an opportunistic thief, chances are a thirty-year-old coat would be the last thing he'd be after, but she was keeping it close all the same.

She could keep hold of it, the head woman had said. Nice coat like that should be returned to its rightful owner fair and square. Tessa's mother would have wanted her to have it.

Not the best way to go about it then, chucking it out with the rubbish only for it to get passed from pillar to post until years later it had surfaced amongst the jumble of the clothing exchange.

But Tessa knew her mother had done no such thing. If she'd truly shared the same passion for making her own clothes, she'd not have made a coat of this quality and felt anything but pride. Far more likely it'd have been left hanging in her wardrobe the day she died, which meant there was only one possible culprit who'd consigned it, along with everything else she'd owned, to the dustbin, pawn shop, a ruthless market trader perhaps.

For all Tessa knew, this coat might be the very least her mother had wanted her to inherit. Nothing of value — at least not in shillings and pence — but perhaps other pieces she'd sewn herself and was duly proud of, or some sort of trinket — an ornament she'd been fond of or a photograph of them as a family, perhaps ... whatever her mother's wishes for the child she'd loved after all, Tessa would never know for sure, since Esme Lane had taken it upon herself to ride roughshod all over them.

And she'd taken something far more precious still. All these years she'd led Tessa to believe she'd not been loved by her own mother, that it had been her own fault she'd had to be foisted upon the Lanes' charity.

Serve her right, it would, if Tessa returned home now only to collect her belongings and then slept on Dorrie's couch until such a time as she could move into Hockley Street. Serve Esme Lane right if her past misdemeanours came back to haunt her and she was left to fend for herself.

But like she'd told Dorrie, Tessa would do no such thing. Even now, as dazed and bewildered as she felt, she'd not for one minute turn her back on the old lady.

Out of loyalty to Hillie, and more so, to Matthew.

Tears pricked Tessa's eyelids as she wandered aimlessly along, arms around the bundle under her coat as if she were cradling a newborn babby.

Her head ached with what she'd found

out tonight and her instinct, as ever, was to confide in Matthew. She wanted to be able to tell him, like she'd always told him everything.

Until they'd got married she had, at any rate. Since he'd put that ring on her finger, it had all gone wrong.

Tessa stopped walking, lifting her face up to the sky where the stars twinkled in the darkness. Was Matthew looking up at that very same sky? Or was he up there, flying through it?

'No matter how far away I am, we'll always be under the same sky,' he'd told her before he'd left that first time, and he'd smiled at her. 'You'll not miss me, Tess, but if you do, just remember we'll both be looking up at the very same stars.'

'I do miss you, Matthew Lane,' she whispered now, her gaze fixed on the stars overhead. 'I miss you, I love you, and I wish you were here with me.'

In an instant the darkness was splintered by the far reaching beams of the searchlights criss-crossing the sky, followed almost immediately by the wail of the air raid siren.

Dazed still, Tessa's feet remained frozen to the spot, but then she thought of Matthew and how she'd never see him again if she was caught by a bomb out here in the street, and so she broke into a run.

Esme's house was two minutes away, but then she'd have to get her out into the shelter ...

The siren was still wailing as she hurtled along the side of the house but as she fumbled all fingers and thumbs to unlock the door, it stopped abruptly, the sudden silence roaring in her ears.

She knew what that meant. They had only minutes to get into the shelter before the planes droned overhead.

In her armchair, Esme sat stiffly, resolute in her determination to stay put in her Arthur's house.

'You'll not get me in that shelter,' she declared straightaway. 'I'd not waste your energy if I were you. Get yerself down there if you must, but leave me be.'

'I'm going in it, and I'm taking you with me,' Tessa said firmly. 'And I've no intention of copping it on your account so you'd best get up, hadn't you?'

Forcing herself to take deep breaths, Tessa retrieved her mother's coat out from under her own. She had to think clearly — there was no chance she'd get Esme up and out of that chair if she didn't have both hands to do it with.

'I'm telling you, I'm not setting one foot in that there hole in the ground,' Esme persisted, but Tessa heard the tremble in her voice and she renewed her efforts to hoist the old lady onto her feet.

'You've no need to fret,' she muttered. 'We'll be safe as houses in there.'

'Safe as houses, is it?' Esme echoed in disbelief. 'Might as well sit it out in my Arthur's armchair, then!'

For all her defiance Esme was frightened, Tessa thought. No other reason why she'd lean on Tessa to so much as go to the privy, let alone to the end of the garden. With her ageing joints it was a slow journey, every second of which Tessa's ears were straining to listen for the tell-tale drone of bombers approaching.

In the nick of time she'd got Esme down the steps and into the damp darkness of the shelter, slamming the door shut again between them and the world outside as the first of the planes thundered overhead.

With shaking hands she lit the lamp and in the sudden light Esme's face was pinched with fear.

'Sit yourself down,' Tessa commanded, helping her to settle onto one of the bunks. 'Hillie and me brought things down we might need ... there you go, that'll keep the damp out your bones.' Retrieving a folded blanket from the opposite bunk, she tucked it around Esme's thin shoulders.

'Not me bones I'm frit about,' Esme grumbled. 'My chest that'll take a battering stuck down here for hours on end.' In the dim light her gaze passed. over Tessa and settled on the precious cargo she'd bundled once more under her arm. 'All right for those of us who've got money to be frittering away on new coats — unless you've gone and snaffled it out from under their noses down at that clothing exchange of yours.'

Perched stiffly on the bunk opposite, Tessa regarded her coldly. 'You don't recognise it then? Still, you won't have set eyes on it since you gave away every little thing my mother owned twenty-two years ago.'

With not so much as a blink of surprise, Esme faced her defiantly.

'Your ma's coat then, is it? That'll be why you're sitting there like Lady Muck, looking down yer nose at me when I'd every right to pawn your ma's belongings. Left me no choice, did she? Expecting me to bring up her babby with not a penny put towards it, and my Arthur back from the Great War and struggling with his chest that much it was all he could do to make it to work.'

She shook her head accusingly at Tessa. 'Wasn't enough that you barged your way under his roof and gave him an extra mouth to feed, now you're stopping my Mattie finding a nice, young lass to marry. He only wed you in the first place — soft lad that he is — when I told him it was high time you were out from under my feet and making your own way ... '

'Then you'll be pleased to know I've every intention of doing just that,' Tessa cut in. 'Be happening a bit quicker, it will, too, if your Hillie decides to come back, though for the life of me I can't see what would possess her, and in the meantime do I take it you prefer having me under your feet to going all day every day without so much as a cup of tea?'

New Plans

In her mother's coat, Tessa walked briskly along Hockley Street, the finished nylon blouses she'd been running up of an evening over the past week draped over her arm, a yard of muslin protecting them from ending up infused with the scent of factory smoke.

It'd not be too long now before she'd be making up all her designs at Hockley Street, but while she and Lil remained at Ambrose's, the time they could devote to furnishing and preparing the premises limited to weekends, the evenings she'd not been on duty at the Town Hall she'd willingly spent working on an initial supply of garments she hoped would tempt their eventual customers.

Between the factory, setting up the business with Lil, her WVS commitments and looking after Esme, Tessa had not a moment to herself until her head hit the pillow, at which point she tended to be so worn out that she'd be asleep in minutes, but it was a relief to have every moment of every day filled with no possibility of dwelling on how frightened she was for Matthew.

For weeks now the skies had played host to battle after battle, Matthew's part in it clear from the scarcity of his letters. The odd one that did arrive, still addressed to the Lane Family, was brief and devoid of the warmth with which he'd written to Tessa. Reading between the lines, desperate for reassurance that he was coping, Tessa felt as though she was reading the words of a stranger.

She'd not written to him, and not once had he questioned it. As much as it hurt her to consider it, she was beginning to think that Matthew was relieved she'd clearly worked out for herself that their marriage was nothing more than he'd always claimed — just a way of keeping Tessa's feet firmly under his ma's table.

Esme herself had said as much those first few hours they'd spent in the shelter. Used to the old lady's cutting comments,

Tessa had initially dismissed it as more of the same, but when she'd thought about it later, the whole thing had the ring of truth about it.

Quite probable that Esme had told *her Mattie* in no uncertain terms that it was high time Tessa was out and making her own way in the world, and just like Matthew to go and marry her rather than see her out on the streets.

He knew that in her job she'd not be called up but he'd given her that as a reason so he'd not have to tell her that Esme wanted rid of her.

So much the better for Esme Lane that she'd not got her own way, Tessa reflected grimly. Be in a bit of a fix now if she had, wouldn't she?

Though Hilary might not have left her if she'd not had Tessa to rely on, when as it was, she'd been in Wales with Granny Peg and Victoria for over a month.

Aside from a brief letter to say she'd arrived safely, they'd heard nothing from her since. Tessa was convinced she'd been right to suspect that Hilary had no intention of returning to Birmingham, but if Esme feared the same, outwardly she hid it, declaring on a daily basis she'd be expecting her Hillie back through the door any day now …

That first night without her, when she'd had to depend on Tessa to help her out to the shelter, had shaken Esme up a fair bit, not that she'd admit to it in a month of Sundays.

Tessa had been frightened herself, listening to the drone of the planes over their heads and waiting to heat the whistle and crunch of bombs dropping around them. The market hall had copped it that first raid, Mary's haberdashery stall and the rest of them gone in one night, leaving nothing but smoking rafters the following morning.

Green's had been caught up in the blast too. Never again would Tessa and Lil while away their Saturday afternoons over a pot of tea and a custard slice, but with every spare hour they had given to setting up the business, in truth they'd not had time to miss it.

A Homecoming

Once their Saturday morning shift at Ambrose's was over, Lil went straight home to Hockley Street, and Tessa went with her, the rest of the day spent painting walls, polishing shelves and the like, but today Lil had gone on ahead to knock them up a spot of lunch while Tessa called in Esme's house to pick up the finished blouses.

After spending precious minutes brewing up a pot of tea and making Esme some lunch, Tessa quickened her step as she walked the last few yards to Lil and Bertie's front door.

Letting herself in, she hung her mother's coat up carefully on the hook by the door, just as Lil's voice floated through from the sitting room.

'Tea in the pot, Tess!'

With the blouses draped for the moment over a kitchen chair, Tessa poured herself a cup of tea, before heading through to the sitting room where Lil was armed with a duster and polishing the gilt frame of their new full-length mirror.

Setting down her duster for a minute, she wiped her hands on her pinny before holding them out for the new blouses.

'Let's have a look, then. You sit yourself down five minutes and get that tea down you before you so much as pick up a needle and thread.'

'Two minutes will do.' Tessa smiled at her as she perched on the edge of the armchair to drink her tea and eat the sandwich Lil had made for her. 'Those mannequins want dressing.'

Lil glanced at the pair of polished wood mannequins that were to stand in the front window, dolled up sufficiently to capture the interest of passing trade and entice them in through the door.

'Don't look to me as though they'll freeze if they've to wait another five minutes,' she chided Tessa. 'You on the other hand will be meeting yourself coming back if you keep this pace up.

How's our Esme today?'

'Swathed in more blankets than a babby and totting up all the times I run off and leave her with nothing more than a pot of tea and a roaring fire,' Tessa replied wryly. 'If Hillie ever walks back through that door, she'll need another month just to listen to Esme's tales of how she's suffered without her.'

'She's done all right out of it,' Lil declared bluntly. 'Pawning all your mother's things like that, just to feather her own nest, she's no right to expect you to give two hoots for her, Tess.'

'I don't think she does expect it,' Tessa pondered. 'Hilary walking out on her has knocked her for six and if her own daughter can turn her 'back on her like that, what's to stop the glorified lodger doing the same? Reckon she's just waiting for the day when I pack my bags and leave her to it.'

'She'd not have a leg to stand on if you did,' Lil sighed, her attention turning to the blouses on her lap, and the delicate stitching that was the trademark of both

Tessa and her mother before her. 'This cream blouse is the one, Tess. If we team it with the brown checked skirt, we'll have one of them mannequins looking a treat.'

Tessa nodded thoughtfully, seeing the proposed outfit in her mind's eye as she finished her sandwich.

'Then we should have the other one in a dress. That pale blue cotton one with the lavender floral print, maybe? What do you think?'

'I think it'd be topped off nicely by the lilac silk scarf,' Lil suggested, looking pointedly at Tessa. 'Times as they are, I know we've no chance of getting anything like the amount of silk we'd need for a batch of follow-up orders but there's no point holding back the scarves you've made already, is there? Folk want a bit of glamour, Tess — cheers them up.'

'Price of that silk, I'll not get in the way of anyone happy to reimburse us for it,' Tessa conceded. 'Round here though, Lil, we're catering to the housewife end of the market, aren't we? Women and girls who've got a spare bit of money to buy themselves something nice that'll not cost the earth — they're how we'll make a go of all this.'

Lil nodded. 'And you want Tessa Lane originals in the window that'll not have them scurrying past for fear they've not enough in their purses to so much as cross the threshold.' She smiled as she pushed a plate of cakes across the table towards Tessa.

'Have a cake before you're up and at it. You know, you've inherited a fair bit more than just your name, Tess. Way Dorrie tells it, before she and your ma got ideas of flitting off to Paris, it were the everyday folk of Brum for whom the first Tessa Thorne took up her needle and thread.'

A pride in her mother's achievements that grew with every anecdote Dorrie remembered made Tessa smile as she returned her empty cup to the table.

'She was well known for it by all accounts.'

'As will you be,' Lil predicted confidently. 'With that in mind, I've the perfect name for our shop.'

'Hope it's nicer than *The Rag Bag*,' Tessa grinned. 'Not one of Bertie's better ideas, that.'

'He's a cheeky so and so,' Lil agreed, but the sparkle in her eye faded a little as she looked at Tessa, clearly unsure of how her suggestion Would be received.

'Thing is, Tess, there'll be a fair few round here who remember your mother and the talent she had — I think it'd be nice to announce to the world that you're Tessa Thorne's daughter and every bit as talented.' She hesitated, sitting forward to take Tessa's hand in hers before she continued.

'What do you think to calling ourselves *L'il Tessa's*? As in little Tessa, but abbreviated so I'm up there with you too?'

Her chest swelling with pride, for both her mother and herself, Tessa swallowed the lump in her throat as she squeezed Lil' s hand.

'I think that's perfect,' she said softly. 'Absolutely perfect.'

Lil beamed with relief. 'We'll have a sign painted. Give Matthew a bit of a clue when he's tracking you down,' she added, the twinkle firmly back in her eye. 'Course, you could write and save him the trouble.'

'I've mannequins to dress,' Tessa retorted, getting briskly to her feet. 'And you've no time to be picking on me when that mirror wants polishing, Mrs Cooper.'

In truth it did help to keep her spirits up when Lil talked of Matthew's return like it was a certainty. Tessa herself had clung to the same belief all this time and she'd continue to do so until the war was over and he'd come home safely, but knowing he was up there, flying into danger time and time again, she couldn't help but be afraid.

But Lil talked of when Matthew came back, not if, and no matter how Tessa despaired of her friend's inability to understand that things between her and Matthew were not how she imagined, her heart lifted every time.

'Way it's looking with you, Hilary, I'd not be surprised if Matthew beats her back here,' Lil pondered, and yet again she was every inch the voice of authority so that when Tessa glanced up from dressing the first of the mannequins in the same instant as they heard footsteps outside, for a fleeting second she was convinced the owner of them was Matthew himself.

'Expecting someone else, were you, Tess?' Bertie enquired, and Lil smiled as she glimpsed his reflection in the polished mirror.

'She'll be expecting someone else til the day he walks back through that door.'

Bertie looked solemnly at Tessa. 'Not Matthew that's turned up out of the blue, but you'd best get home anyway. Hilary's back, Tess. She's been in the Black Horse looking for you.'

A Sad Return

Hilary had come back. Over a month spent in the relatively safe surroundings of the Welsh countryside with the daughter she loved so much, and a landlady in Granny Peg who'd clearly no objection to suddenly being lumbered with yet another member of the Lane family, and Hilary had chosen to return to the smoky, industrial target of Birmingham, where there'd already been bombings and no guarantee there'd not be more still.

Even if her conscience had brought her back to Esme's side, it had kept her there minutes only before she'd been off scouring the Black Horse for signs of Tessa. An hour if that since Tessa had left Esme alone in the house — for Hillie to have returned and dashed out again in that time when she'd not seen her ma for weeks on end, whatever she had to say to Tessa was clearly of the utmost urgency.

Was it to do with Matthew? Had

Hilary been writing to him? The scarcity of his letters was perhaps not just down to the pace of life on Dover air base, but also because he'd been alternating them with letters to his sister — the one member of the family who'd written to him in return.

That would be why Hilary was back. Of course she'd be of no mind to listen to Esme's tales of woe when she'd every intention of catching the last train back to Wales this evening. Only as a messenger was she here, the purpose of such a fleeting visit to seek out Tessa and impart the news she understood only too well would break her heart. That'd be why Bertie had looked so solemn.

Something had happened to Matthew.

It hadn't, it couldn't have. Esme's address would be the one the Air Force had on file if they'd needed to send such a letter. Tessa was down as his next of kin.

She'd know if … well, she'd know.

Sheer terror all the same catapulted her into a frantic run from Hockley

Street to Esme's house, where she burst through the back door to find only Esme looking more withered than ever in her Arthur's armchair.

Of Hilary there was no sign, but her suitcase was propped up by the table. Not just a case of there and back in a day then. Perhaps she'd come back for good after all, and her haste to track down Tessa borne of nothing more than an anxiety to be reacquainted after the weeks they'd spent apart.

Adrenalin giving way to exhaustion that made her legs tremble, Tessa sank gratefully into a chair, forcing herself to speak calmly.

'Hillie's back, then?'

'Not so you'd know it,' Esme mumbled. 'Here one minute, flitting off again the next Seems she's a list as long as yer arm of things she's to see to before she'll spare a word or two for her own ma. She's more to say to you than me.'

But the gaze she fixed on Tessa was not accusing so much as wistful. 'Straight out looking for you, she was.'

'Did she say what was so urgent?' Tessa asked quietly, the quiver in her voice not going undetected by Esme, though she mistook the cause of it.

'You've every need to look worried, my girl. Waltzed off down the Corporation she has — putting her name down for a house, if you please. Reckons she'll be moved up the list as she's got our Vic.' Esme looked wryly at Tessa, but there was a tremble in her own voice that for once she made no attempt to conceal, or maybe she was just unable to do so. 'Know what that means, don't yer? She'll be off and you'll be left here with me til they cart me off in a box.'

'Outlive us all, you will.' Wearily, Tessa got to her feet. 'I'd best brew us up a pot of tea, then, hadn't I?'

Hilary was after setting herself up in her own home then. No wonder she'd left her suitcase propped up by the table — no sense in unpacking when she'd no intention of stopping under Esme's roof.

Not that it'd be that quick. There'd be

a waiting list, and with Victoria at present evacuated with Granny Peg, Tessa couldn't see that Hilary's case would be considered a priority.

It wouldn't matter, though. Even if she had to wait months or more to be allocated a house, just knowing that she'd eventually be bringing Victoria back to their own home together, with no Esme grumbling the odds every five minutes, Hilary would be more at peace than she'd been in a long time.

Not so for Tessa, left as she would be to run around after Esme for the rest of her days, but as she stood in the small kitchen, leaning heavily on the worktop as she waited for the pot to boil, she felt so weak with relief that it didn't seem to matter. If she'd hurtled home to be told that she'd have to spend every waking minute with Esme from now on, as long as Matthew was alive and safe she'd see it as a small price to pay.

But Hilary wouldn't see it that way. Yet to be told of the consuming fear that had propelled Tessa home so fast it had been luck more than judgement that she'd stayed on two feet, Hilary would be thinking only of the enormity of the responsibility she'd be expecting Tessa to shoulder, and she'd be wanting to track her down and explain before she got wind of it from someone else.

Shame Esme had beaten her to it, Tessa thought, one eye on the clock as the hours passed with no sign of Hilary. She'd be caught up at the Housing Corporation, but for this long?

Were it not for the suitcase standing by the table, Tessa might have suspected her sister-in-law had flitted off back to Wales until such a time as she had her own house to come home to.

She'd cooked their tea and had hers and Esme's on the table by the time Hilary eventually appeared.

'Bit of a wait, were it?' Esme queried, but it was Tessa at whom Hilary glanced remorsefully as she replied quietly.

'In and out as it happens, but I'd other things to do as well. I'm sorry I missed you before, Tess.' Taking up a plate, she spooned out the stew Tessa had left warming for her in the pan. 'I've that much to tell you — most of it from Victoria. Them kittens of hers are right little scallywags — into everything, they are ... '

It took Tessa seconds to understand that, as determined as Hilary was to take herself and Victoria out from under Esme's roof, when it came to talking of her plans in her ma's hearing, her conscience pulled her up.

With Esme no more inclined to talk of the day when her Hillie would finally fly the nest, the subject was left alone until a bit later when Esme fell to dozing in her chair, her mind eased by Hilary's presence, for now at least.

'You had me convinced you'd not be coming back,' Tessa ventured, as Hilary poured them each a fresh cup of tea. 'All your worldly possessions crammed into that suitcase — I thought you'd be buying a one-way ticket.'

Hilary looked straight at her. 'I did, Tess. When I left that day, I'd no intention of returning. All I wanted was to be with Victoria. I couldn't think past that.'

'You were in a lot of pain, Hillie.' Tessa rested her hand briefly over hers.

'You'd every right to time with your daughter. What's this Granny Peg like, then?'

'Every bit as nice as we'd been led to believe,' Hilary sighed. 'I'd barely got my coat off and she were pouring me tea. Evenings we spent talking about my Leo ... she listened to every word, Tess. Told me eventually how she's lost loved ones herself. Two daughters she had, and both of them gone before her.'

She swallowed hard. 'Easy to see she's a hole in her life Victoria fills, but I'm of no mind to take offence, Tess. If you could see how settled Victoria is there, how at ease she is living somewhere she's no need to watch every word she says, I'll not condemn Peg for giving my daughter the chance to live like that, and for reminding me how important it is that I give her the same chance when she comes home.'

'Why you were straight out and down

the Corporation,' Tessa exclaimed softly, and Hilary nodded.

'She's had to tiptoe round Ma her whole life. I'll not bring her back here to more of the same.' For once her hazel eyes glinted as fiercely as Matthew's.

'I've lost my Leo, Tess. I'll not lose Victoria as well.'

Tessa squeezed her hand. 'He'd be proud of you, Hillie. You know he would.'

She smiled sadly. 'He'd say it'd took me long enough, wouldn't he? I just wish he knew I'd been ready to walk out that door with him the moment he walked back through it.'

'You'll be doing it for him,' Tessa said gently. 'You and Victoria.'

'Time we were off, anyway,' Hilary declared bravely. 'This house isn't big enough for all of us. Once Matthew's home safe and sound, you'll be wanting to have your own family.'

Tessa looked away from her. 'It's not like that,' she mumbled. 'Not with us. First thing Matthew will be wanting to do is get us both back down that register office so we can put a stop to all this.'

'You love him, don't you?' Hilary pointed out, as if it were that simple, and Tessa forced herself to meet her gaze, swallowing back the tears.

'Lot of good it did me telling him like that. He's not written a word to me since.'

Hilary looked thoughtful as she sipped her tea. 'He'll have plenty to say, Tess. Maybe he's just saving it til he sees you again. Maybe some things are too precious ... '

She stopped abruptly as the whine of the air raid siren shattered the stillness, her hazel eyes pools of fear as she gripped Tessa's sleeve.

'It's all right, Hillie,' Tessa reassured her. 'We've time to get Esme out to the. shelter.'

At the mention of her ma, Hilary seemed to spring into action, but it was to Tessa she looked to take over rousing Esme from her doze, and to get all three of them down the garden in time.

This would be the first air raid Hilary

had been caught up in, Tessa reasoned.

She'd been similarly bewildered herself that first night, back in August, when they'd flattened the Market Hall. Hilary had gone to Wales that very morning, escaping the bombers by the skin of her teeth, but her first night back in Birmingham and the sky was thick with a swann of planes.

It was almost as if they'd been holding on for Hilary's return, Tessa pondered grimly when the following night had them once more scrambling down the garden and into the shelter.

For a while Birmingham had been left in peace but it was almost as if the bombers had followed Hilary home.

'You'll not be getting me back in that there hole for love nor money,' Esme declared, each time the rise and fall of the siren pierced her evening doze. 'Way that damp sits on my chest, it'll not be them bombs finishing me off. Be no less safe in my Arthur's armchair.'

Both determined they'd not be taking their chances huddled under the table, between them Tessa and Hilary had Esme up and out of her chair and down the steps into the shelter before the planes droned overhead.

As a defence against the damp air that did indeed circulate within the confines of the shelter, Esme was tucked up in the warmest blankets they had and kept supplied with hot tea from the thermos flask.

History dictated such tasks to be Hilary's domain but Tessa found it was herself to whom Esme looked for assistance. It was perhaps down to the hours they'd spent in the shelter previously; with Hilary in Wales, Esme had been left with only Tessa when the whole city had suddenly seemed to shake with the crunch of bombs dropping around them.

More likely, though, it was down to the indifference Hilary showed to Tessa effectively stepping into her shoes.

Night after night of sitting for hours in the shelter, her nerves as tight as a bow-string, Tessa quickly felt as if she were walking round in a haze, but although

Hilary was similarly pale-faced with exhaustion, it was clear to see that the thought of her new home, and the new, unencumbered existence she'd lead with Victoria back by her side, lifted her spirits and distracted her mind from the nightly explosions.

They'd yet to talk of Hilary's move in Esme's hearing, and the old lady herself, though she'd doubtless have a fair bit to say about it, had left the subject well alone, but she knew all the same her days of having her Hillie by her side were numbered.

Lulled into a fitful doze one night, Tessa was jolted awake again by the sudden crunch of a bomb outside and in the dim lamplight she saw the sad, defeated look in Esme's eyes as she watche:d Hilary sleeping opposite. Her gaze passing over on to Tessa; Esme managed the faintest of smiles.

'Make a decent flask of tea, I'll say that for you. Suppose my Mattie could do worse.'

Genuine affection it wasn't but it was

the closest she'd be likely to get, Tessa surmised, pulling her mother's coat tightly around her.

Two weeks of night after night in the shelter and for the moment Birmingham was left in peace, but the city Tessa loved was broken. Her own home, and the house on Hockley Street, Dorrie's place too, were all in one piece, but she'd no chance now of walking to work, or to see Lil, or even down the road to the shop, without passing blackened shells of houses or piles of brick and splintered furniture where once a house had stood.

With half the city rendered homeless, she couldn't see that there'd be a house spare for Hilary to rent any time soon, but perhaps she'd reckoned without the stalwart spirit Brum folk had in abundance for picking themselves up, dusting themselves off and getting on with it as normal, because it was but a week or two afterwards that Hilary received a letter informing her she'd been allocated a house for her and her daughter.

'You'll be off then, will you?' were the

first words Esme had spoken on the subject since the day Hilary had gone off to put her name down, but she'd no more chance of burying her head in the sand, Tessa thought, not when Hilary was standing there with the letter clutched in her hand.

Now it had come down to it though, Hilary's conscience was troubling her.

Two weeks of bombs dropping around them and she was off and leaving her ma when for years she'd looked after her round the clock ... and in doing so, she'd more than made up for the callous way in which Arthur Lane had turned from his wife, Tessa thought fiercely, as she reached her arm around Hilary's shoulders.

'You're to take that house, Hillie. I'll be here to keep your ma in tea leaves. You've no need to fret.' She smiled wryly. 'Besides, they'll not dare drop bombs on Esme's head.'

'Too busy dropping them on Coventry instead,' Esme piped up. 'Razed to the ground last night, it were. Stone's throw from Brum and all — they'll be having another go at us next, you mark my words.'

She was shaken up by the raids, her fear that this war was flying all too close once more apparent in the way she clung for a moment to Hilary's hand.

She'd stop one more night, Hilary decided, and Tessa could see how it eased her mind to be doing so. What did one more night matter? From tomorrow onwards she'd be settled in her new home, ready for when Victoria came back to stay for Christmas.

With the keys in her possession however, Hilary was reluctant to leave her house uninhabited for a moment.

'Will you stop there tonight, Tess? Get the place aired for me and have that pot on to boil for when I move in tomorrow?'

It would make a nice change, Tessa thought. Once her shift at the Town Hall was finished, she'd have an hour or two to work on her sewing with no Esme clamouring for a fresh brew every five minutes. If she put her mind to it, those plaid skirts that were the last of the pre-liminary pieces to be displayed in *L'il Tessa's* she'd have hemmed and button-holed by tomorrow, ready for when she and Lil opened their doors in time for the run up to Christmas ...

In the cold, grey light of early morning, she retraced her steps back to Esme's house, her mind focused on picking up her feet so she'd not stand on the hoses that wound their way in all directions, dribbling water into damp — smelling pools of charred plaster and brick dust.

If she took care to step over the splintered glass that crunched underfoot she'd not have to look up and see the shells of houses that had been blown to bits, or the rescue squads digging tirelessly through the rubble, the covered stretchers being carried quietly away.

'Tess! Oh, Tess!' Out of nowhere she found herself looking into the white face of Lil, who grabbed her and held her tightly, before turning to call over her shoulder 'Bertie! She's here! She's all right!'

Why wouldn't she be?

Lil's voice sounded distant, like she was hearing it underwater.

'Come on, Tess. Dorrie's manning the canteen — we'd best get you a cup of tea.'

'In a minute,' Tessa managed. 'Hillie ... I've to take her key ...'

Lil's hand tightened on her arm, and then Bertie was there too, his arm atound her shoulders physically turning her away from the smouldering remains of the house she'd lived in her whole life.

Her teeth chattering, Tessa pulled her mother's coat tightly around her, the closest she'd ever come to being wrapped in her arms.

A Longed-For Reply

December 1940

A dense fog hung heavily on the air as Tessa reached for Victoria's gloved hand and held it tightly. Long since familiar with every corner of this remote Welsh village, there was little chance of Victoria losing her way, even with the world so thickly shrouded it was all they could do to see past the end of their noses, but Tessa had seen too many she loved lost to her, and she tightened her hold on her niece's hand, their footsteps echoing in the stillness as they walked to the post office.

They had Christmas cards to post, to Lil and Bertie back in Birmingham, to Dorrie and to Bea, who'd managed to get herself a bit of leave so she could spend Christmas with her ma. On the day itself they'd all be together, as a family, to which Tessa and Victoria belonged. Lil especially had been falling over herself to have them both at Hockley Street, but for this year at least Tessa felt a quiet Christmas with Granny Peg and her brood of kittens would be best for Victoria.

It was for Victoria that she'd made the effort to write and post Christmas cards at all. If it was down to her, she'd forget all about Christmas this year, but it seemed important that she kept things as normal as she could, although in truth Victoria was in no cheerier spirits — it was perhaps because of this she should post the cards, buy presents and help Granny Peg to string up every last fairy light.

If the Coopers were family, then through Lil's marriage to Bertie, so too was Granny Peg. It had been a few weeks now since Lil had accompanied Tessa on the train to Wales, vowing she'd not leave her side until such time as she and Victoria wished to be left alone to grieve for Hillie, and for Esme too, but even in a memory clouded by pain and tears, Tessa could still picture Lil's face when they'd been met off the train by Granny Peg.

They'd had no reason to put two and two together; Hillie had told Tessa how Granny Peg had lost two daughters, how it was her granddaughter's room she'd be making up for Hillie, but even though she knew Margaret Foster could well be shortened to Granny Peg, the penny hadn't dropped.

Not until the moment Lil had stepped off the train and, perhaps because she'd seen Tessa robbed of half her family in one night, tears she'd likely held back since she'd first arrived in Birmingham had spilled down her face as she'd flown into her grandmother's arms.

Lil had written regularly, both to Tessa and to Granny Peg. She and Bertie would be down for a few days in the New Year, she promised. Bertie was itching to play Peg's grand piano and perhaps they could have a bit of a sing-song, try and raise Victoria's spirits. Proudly she'd relayed their plans for *Li'l Tessa's* to her grandmother, who'd declared her intention to travel up to Birmingham and buy a *L'il Tessa* original for herself.

She'd have to be quick if Lil was right in predicting that with Christmas looming, every last garment would fly off the shelves. As yet, Tessa's sewing machine had remained idle. She'd no new ideas for designs and no energy to sit down and think of any.

A piercing whistle shattered the silence, announcing the arrival of a train into the little country station and startling Victoria, who huddled closer to Tessa as the sound echoed eerily in the thick fog.

'My cats don't like it when the trains whistle,' she confided quietly. 'Scrapes runs and hides under my bed, but Hazel's a bit braver, she leaps up on the windowsill to see what's going on, then she sits there keeping watch til the train goes away.'

'She's looking after you,' Tessa told her. 'Making sure the train's not after having you for its dinner.'

Victoria managed a thin smile. 'She's the one I named after Ma, 'cause of Ma's hazel eyes, see.'

'I know, bab.'Tessa squeezed her close. 'That's why she looks after you.'

Victoria nodded. 'Sometimes I pretend Hazel is Ma come back to me as a cat. Do you think that's silly, Tess?'

'I think if she's found a way to do that she'll be sitting on your windowsill right this minute, washing her paws.'

'She always kept everything clean. Remember how we were making that snowman and Ma was cleaning out the stove ... ' Victoria's voice trembled. 'Ma and Pa, they'll be looking after each other now, won't they, Tess?'

'Course they will.'

'Granny, too,' Victoria continued. 'She'll be wanting her tea brewed and Pa will be grumbling 'cause of Ma waiting on Granny but really he won't mind 'cause they'll be there together.'

Tessa stopped walking, turning to Victoria, whose watery eyes looked to hers for reassurance.

'I think that's exactly how it'll be.'

'Granny needed Ma to go with her,'

Victoria whispered. 'Like she always needed her, and I didn't mind 'cause there was you and Uncle Matthew, and I weren't left on my own ...' Her voice caught in a hastily suppressed sob.

'What'll happen to me now, Tess? When I come home, where will I live?'

Tessa grasped her shoulders. 'You listen to me, Victoria. Soon as it's safe you'll come back and you'll live with me and Aunty Lil and Uncle Bertie, in our new house above the shop, all right? I'm your aunty, and I love you. We'll live together, I promise.'

Victoria smiled bravely, blinking back the tears, some of which nonetheless spilled down her cheeks.

'Uncle Matthew too,' she prodded. 'He'll be all right 'cause I found that lucky penny to keep him safe.'

'Then he'd best get himself home in one piece, hadn't he?' Tessa forced a smile as she linked her arm through Victoria's. 'And you and me had best get cracking. We'll miss the post, else.'

She couldn't tell Victoria that the

precious lucky penny she'd kept safely stowed away in a drawer all these months had been lost for ever the night the house collapsed, burying the drawer and its contents in a pile of rubble so deep she'd known there was no chance of finding a tiny muslin pouch amongst it.

No more than she could bear to dwell on what it meant herself — losing something on which, foolishly or not, she'd placed such value. If she kept the penny safe, then in turn Matthew would be safe too.

She should have put it in her pocket the night she'd gone to stop over at Hilary's house — but then she shouldn't have been going anywhere to begin with.

Fate had decreed that Hilary received the keys to her first real home the morning before the only one she'd ever known was bombed to pieces. If she'd just stood firm against her ma and moved out then and there, she'd have been spared and Victoria would not have lost her mother. Matthew wouldn't be coming home eventually to find he'd lost his sister.

Looking after Esme had become Tessa's responsibility. It should have been Tessa they'd eventually uncovered, huddled under the table with an old lady so worn down from long, cold nights in a damp shelter that she'd finally dug her heels in, knowing she'd a far better chance of getting her own way with her Hillie.

That bomb had been meant for Tessa, until the last minute twist of fate that had taken Hilary away from her daughter for ever.

Glancing through the envelopes to ensure she'd not forgotten any as they waited behind the counter at the post office, Tessa's gaze rested a little longer on the one addressed to Dover Air Base,

She'd known she'd have to write and tell Matthew. First thing she'd thought, sitting there with a blanket tucked around her shoulders and a cup of tea placed gently into her hand while to all sides of her rescue workers were digging through the rubble, she'd have to tell Matthew.

She needed him to come back and be with her. For a while, though, she'd not found the words. How could she tell him that he'd lost his mother and his sister, and that it was her fault Hillie was gone?

As much as she needed him to come back. she didn't deserve him to.

'No more than Matthew deserves to find out from anyone but you,' Lil had chided her gently. 'Tess, he needs to know and he needs you to tell him. Same as you need him to be here with you.'

Still she'd put it off, concentrating instead on Victoria, but as Christmas loomed, there was a chance Matthew might have some leave — she couldn't bear for him to go back to Birmingham expecting to find them all and instead finding nothing but a pile of dust. Not when she wouldn't be there to catch him.

But the letter she'd eventually written had been brief. She'd just scribbled down Granny Peg's address, told him she needed to see him and to find her there.

He'd know something was wrong, but

at least she could save him having to read the words.

Lil was right — Matthew should hear it from Tessa, but in person rather than a few lines in an envelope.

Christmas cards despatched, and Matthew's letter winging its way to Dover, Tessa lifted the latch on Grahny Peg's back gate, she and Victoria slipping through quickly so as not to let this year's litter of kittens stray beyond the safety of the garden.

Reassured that after the war she'd be returning to live with what remained of her family, Victoria's spirits were a little lighter as she checked with Tessa that she'd time yet before dinner to stop outside and play with the kittens.

She'd take her out a cup of tea, Tessa decided. Post office and back in this damp and drizzly fog and she'd not say no to one herself, but as she turned to walk into the cottage, Granny Peg appeared at the back door.

'You've a visitor, Tess,' she said quietly, taking her hand gently in hers.

'Told me to give you this, he did.'

Tessa stared at her palm, and the tiny muslin pouch Granny Peg had placed there. Stained a little by months of brick dust but she'd no need to look inside for the lucky penny to know this was hers. The very same muslin pouch she'd stitched the night Matthew had first left, as closely guarded in her drawer as it had been, the pouch that no-one in the world but she and Matthew knew existed.

Matthew was here.

Granny Peg patted her shoulder kindly. 'I'll get the pot on to boil, take young Victoria a cup if she's after playing with them kittens. You get yourself in that front room quick as there's someone you're a bit keen to see, m'duck.'

Tessa found her voice for long enough to whisper her thanks before her feet took over, propelling her through the kitchen and into the hall so fast she felt as though she'd flown there, and towards the front room, where Matthew was, but he beat her to it, opening the door himself and coming out into the hall, closing his arms tightly around her when she flew into them.

'Tess,' he exclaimed softly, as if he couldn't quite believe his own eyes, and knowing how that felt because she felt the same, Tessa forced herself to step back far enough that she could look him over.

'Are you all right?' she whispered, and he nodded.

'Still in one piece, yes.'

He looked tired though, she noticed. Shadows under his eyes and a face pale from nowhere near enough sleep ... and from the shock of going back to Birmingham only to find he'd lost his family.

She'd not written to him in time. She'd not saved him from facing it alone.

'Oh, Matthew.' She tightened her arms around him once more — 'I'm sorry, I'm so sorry. I should have told you ... '

Matthew gripped her shoulders, holding her at arm's length, and his eyes were fierce though his voice trembled.

'Tess, when I saw the house was gone, I thought ... oh Tess, I thought that was it, I thought I'd lost you.' He swallowed hard. 'My whole family Hillie ... gone just like that ... but it was you, Tess. I couldn't think of anyone but you. When Lil found me and told me you were alive ... I felt like I'd got everything back. One minute I'd lost it and the next I had it all.' His hazel eyes searched hers. 'I'm sorry, too. Way I've treated you, writing every week and then months of nothing ... '

She felt as if the bubble had burst, all the sheer joy of seeing him again dissolving into thin air, as she shook her head quickly.

'It's all right. You've no need to explain anything to me.'

He considered her for a moment. 'I'd say I've every need,' he said softly, taking her hand in his. 'Hear me out, Tess. Please.'

She nodded, and he led her into Granny Peg's front room, where they sat side by side on the couch.

'You know why I was so quick to join up?' he began. 'It was to do with Pa, but it weren't about avenging his death, like

I said it was.' He shook his head in disbelief. 'Might have been if I'd still been thinking of him as some big war hero, if our Hillie hadn't set me straight.'

Tessa reached for his hand. 'I know. She told me too.'

'Way he was with Ma — he broke her heart, he gave her no reason to drag herself out of that chair,' Matthew stated tersely. 'He ruined her life, didn't he? Hillie's too — she'd every right to be up and off with Leo and Victoria, but she was tied to Ma's apron strings til the very end.' He stared down at Tessa's hand in his. 'I went off to do my bit because I wanted to be the man he wasn't.'

'You're not your pa, Matthew,' she said fiercely. 'You're nothing like him.'

He looked up at her. 'Had a fair go at ruining your life, didn't I? Marrying you and five minutes later going off and leaving you ...'

'You've not ruined anything,' Tessa said flatly. 'It was me did that, wasn't it?' She pulled her hand free of his. 'It's all right, Matthew. I know why you didn't write to me.'

'No, you don't, Tess.' He twisted round so he was facing her, though for the moment he made no attempt to reclaim her hand. 'That day we had together, when I was up for Lil and Bertie's wedding, by the time I left I'd convinced myself I'd pushed you into this, and you regretted it, and in that case I'd no right tying you to me when I was going back to fly. I just thought it'd be best if I left you alone,' he finished simply.

'I didn't want to be left alone,' Tessa exclaimed incredulously. How could he think she did? After she'd sent him that letter ... *I love you* ... she couldn't have said it plainer.

'I know that now.' Matthew reached into his pocket, drawing out the envelope she'd sent it in. 'Back then the East Coast was taking a right battering, remember? Sorting office was hit and it's took them this long to redirect the mail. Your letter I've had in my hand less than a week.' He drew a second envelope from his pocket and placed it gently into her hand. 'So I thought I'd better hand deliver my reply, so you're not waiting for it another six months.'

But for a moment Tessa just stared at it, lying innocently in her palm. She was afraid to open it, to read the words she'd been expecting after all these months of no words at all — the words that would break her heart.

'Open it,' Matthew gently urged her. 'Trust me, Tess.'

Her hands were shaking all the same as she unfolded his letter and read the words he'd written in reply.

'*Dear Tess. I love you more. Yours for always, Matthew.*'

She looked up at him, all blurred through the tears she'd kept back all this time. She'd not cried for Esme, she'd not even cried for Hillie; for Victoria's sake, she'd locked it all away inside.

Only to help Victoria come to terms with losing Hillie had she forced herself up and out of bed each morning. Her own pain she felt she'd no right to give way to, and if her sewing machine was left to rust in a cobwebbed corner she'd no energy to care.

But Matthew was here now. Her Matthew, who she loved, and who loved her back, and he didn't blame her for being here when Hillie wasn't. She was near enough all he had left in the world, and she was all the more precious to him because of it.

Matthew reached for both her hands, holding them in his. 'Tess, I didn't marry you to keep you from being called up, nor was it to keep you under Ma's roof, though I know she'll have said as much.' He shuffled closer to her. 'I married you to keep us together, because I love you, Tess. I always have.'

'We'd have stayed together anyway.' Tessa smiled through her tears. 'I'd have let nothing come between you and me. Not even Esme, and if she didn't manage it, the rest of the world's got no chance, have they?'

'None at all,' Matthew agreed, and as he reached his arm around her shoulders, she nestled into him, weak with relief that he was here, and he loved her, and she'd not have to bury the pain of losing their Hillie anymore.

'I love you too much, Matthew.'

'My Tess,' he murmured, holding her tightly. 'It'll be all right now. We'll be all right. You and me, and Victoria. We'll be together, and once this war's over and done with, we'll be staying together.'

'I know we will.' A little calmer now, Tessa lifted her head from Matthew's shoulder, and he smiled at her, leaning in closer to kiss her softly.

'Will It Keep Him Safe?'

Matthew had a week's leave, for which he planned to find a room elsewhere in the village, aware. that he'd be yet another Lane imposing on Granny Peg's hospitality, but she'd not hear of it, insisting that he remain under her roof.

In a cottage that had at one time housed both her daughters, and Lil, too, she'd plenty of room. Chancing upon her humming contentedly as she chopped vegetables for Christmas dinner, Tessa suspected that in truth the old lady preferred her home once more packed to the rafters.

It would have made no odds to Tessa. if she'd spent Christmas with Matthew in the middle of a frozen field. Just having him back by her side was enough. For the first time since she'd been ushered away from the sight of Hillie being carried off on a covered stretcher, she felt so incredibly peaceful.

Matthew would not be returning to Dover. He'd flown that many missions, he'd been told he'd done over and above his bit during the months of constant battles in the air, and the captain had retired him from active service, for the time being at least. Matthew was to start the New Year as a flying instructor on Hawarden training base in Wales.

The relief Tessa felt that he'd be so much closer to home, and spared the greater danger of flying into battle, would perhaps make it a little less painful for her to watch him get back on that train, but she'd worry about that when the time came. First they had a whole week together.

The first light of Christmas morning found Victoria cross-legged on the rag rug by the fire, the glow from the fairy lights she'd helped Tessa to drape around the tree reflected in her hazel eyes as she opened her presents.

'How'd Santa manage that?' she exclaimed softly, peering at the necklace on which was threaded their lucky penny, and Tessa smiled as she fastened the clasp around Victoria's neck.

'With a bit of help from Uncle Matthew, I'd say.'

Closing her fingers protectively around the penny; Victoria looked solemnly at Tessa.

'Will it still keep him safe if I wear it, Tess?'

'It'll look better on you than me, Sprout.' Matthew smiled, reaching around Victoria to hold Tessa's hand. 'How about you wear it for the three, of us?'

'Five of us,' Victoria corrected him, picking up Hazel on to her lap while Scrapes leapt upon the discarded wrapping paper.

'Our little family,' Matthew murmured, his eyes locking with Tessa's as he gently squeezed her hand.

We do hope that you have enjoyed reading this large print book.

Did you know that all of our titles are available for purchase?

We publish a wide range of high quality large print books including:
Romances, Mysteries, Classics
General Fiction
Non Fiction and Westerns

Special interest titles available in large print are:
The Little Oxford Dictionary
Music Book, Song Book
Hymn Book, Service Book

Also available from us courtesy of Oxford University Press:
Young Readers' Dictionary
(large print edition)
Young Readers' Thesaurus
(large print edition)

For further information or a free brochure, please contact us at:
Ulverscroft Large Print Books Ltd.,
The Green, Bradgate Road, Anstey,
Leicester, LE7 7FU, England.
Tel: (00 44) **0116 236 4325**
Fax: (00 44) **0116 234 0205**

Other titles in the
Linford Romance Library:

TURPIN'S APPRENTICE

Sarah Swatridge

England, 1761. Charity Bell is the daughter of an inn keeper. Her two elder sisters are only interested in marrying well, whereas feisty Charity is determined to discover who the culprit is behind the most recent highwayman ambush. And by catching the highwayman, she aims to persuade Sir John to bring his family, and his wealth, to her village. It may also make the handsome Moses notice her!